EVERY CROOKED KINGDOM

A novel by

Alex Katt

Published by Makin Books LLC

Note from the author:

We greatly appreciate you taking the time to read our work. Please consider leaving a review wherever you bought the book, or telling your friends about this book to help us spread the word. Thank you so much for your support.

This book is dedicated to Franklin.
"He is my King and I am his Queen."

CHAPTER ONE

If there's one thing that anyone can learn from paying attention in history class, it's this: you have to be full of shit. If you want to be anyone that is notable, you have to know how to bullshit your way through speeches. Take Hitler, for example. He promoted peace and courage in many of his rants. He convinced his followers that what they were doing was a good thing. And, well, you all know how that turned out.

After 720 days of high school, the school awarded me the most coveted title of all. Valedictorian.

I am smart. I could easily be humble about the whole situation and say that I am just like anybody else in the hick-town of Mountain Hollow, West Virginia, but I tend to be a little on the too-blunt side. (Note that unlike, say, 99 percent of West Virginians, I do pronounce hollow properly. I refuse to say "holler". Every time I apply for another university, I feel as if I am solely and immediately judged by the fact that I am from West Virginia, as if we're all white-trash rednecks who would be detrimental to have on their immaculate campus. Granted, most of us only take one of four paths in life: coalminer, bartender, waitress, or Sunday school teacher. That doesn't give the average person much to work with, or any hope that he'll ever matter to the world in any way. It's kind of depressing to think about. But so it goes.

Anyway, I did what people who have decent life goals do best. On graduation night, after the principal awarded the diplomas and spoke for a few minutes, he called me up to give to the speech for my senior class.

I stood behind the podium and made eye contact with the students and everyone else who was watching me. I waved broadly and smiled at them, and they all cheered. I wasn't even popular. But you didn't have to be to get someone hyped up. "Thank you, thank you!" I said into the microphone. And the room grew quiet again.

In any great speech, alliteration is key. I gave a speech that was nothing but false hope. "This is a wonderful generation of students," I lied. See, bullshit. "We are a group of young people that will produce much success, superiority, and significance. It is an honor to stand before you this evening. I have no doubt that many of us will go on to community colleges and universities and continue to do many great things to make this world a better place." Then I rambled on just a bit. I told a couple stories about my favorite teachers and called out specific students on their most embarrassing moments. And nobody cared. They just laughed and laughed.

"Thank you and have a great night!" I shouted into the mic. I shook hands with the principal. "Good work, son," he said, and patted my back. The two of us shook hands for a few seconds more and smiled so that people could finish taking pictures. There were hundreds of camera flashes from parents who were way too excited.

There were a few closing words and with a toss of our graduation caps, the principal dismissed us for the final time. It was beautiful.

Immediately after the ceremony, my mom, dad, and I were on our merry way to Denny's. Now, before you start dissing my parents for not taking me to the Olive Garden or whatever, Denny's is seriously the nicest restaurant in town. It's the nicest restaurant in any of the surrounding towns, to be honest. Everyone is always trying to convince me that the food at Bertha's Diner is fantastic, but the name alone scares me. That's my grandma's name. She's an awful cook. Well, she was. She died last year. And to this day I swear that I saw the turkey she made on Thanksgiving twitch a bit. Nobody ever believed me.

My mom insisted throughout the whole drive that I wear my cap and gown into the restaurant so that she could take pictures and forever cherish this momentous occasion, which I could have given fewer fucks about. I tried so hard to defend my dignity. "God, Mom. What if I see somebody I know?" Because more than likely, every graduate and their family was going to be there.

"Well they can just get over it. Goodness gracious, my little baby boy is growin' up." She dabbed at her eyes with a (probably used) Kleenex she pulled from her purse, which was more like a gigantic tote bag. The tissue was black when she was done. She wears a lot of makeup. She let the Hollow grow on her much too early in life, so she had absolutely no chance to ever make it. She's a bartender. But just for fun, though, she claims.

"God, Mom. I didn't know it was that important to you." I sighed and died a little inside. "I'll wear it." I know that being embarrassed around the people you were likely never going to see again didn't seem like a big deal, but I wasn't okay with the idea of being remembered that way.

She smiled and stopped crying almost instantly. I swear to effing Jesus she could control that shit. "Thank you, Wade." (Yes, I am named after Wade Hampton. The south loves that guy.)

"You're welcome, Mama." She really likes the rare times I call her that. I mean, I made my mother cry on the proudest moment of her life. It was the least I could do.

My dad pulled into the Denny's parking lot. He told me exactly two words (*congratulations* and *son*) when we left the school, and that's all he wrote. Until now. As we walked into the restaurant he said, "I know that letter from Harvard's coming any day now. I'm damn proud of you."

"Thanks, Dad." You see, he went to Harvard on a full scholarship when he was my age. He was dirt poor but nearly as smart as John Forbes Nash, Jr. himself. (I think they made a movie about that guy.) My dad's good at math. *Very* good. He tutors kids that have to go to summer school to graduate. I don't know why he didn't become a professor. I know I took after him. But I'm more of a literature junkie. Anyway, all he wanted in life was a son (me) to be smart (huzzah) and go to Harvard University just like he did. So, I decided that I was probably going to go. I'm his only kid. I didn't wanna disappoint the man. It's not like he had dreams for me to go to Mountain Holler Community College. That would suck more than the worst thing I could think of...Probably much worse than me wearing my cap and gown to dinner.

The booths in the restaurant were full, so the waitress seated the three of us at a small table not quite in the middle. It still made me a bit uncomfortable to sit there but I couldn't be like, "Excuse me, ma'am, but this table sucks ass. Can you please give my genius self a better seat? Thank you a bunch." That would make me a douche. I don't think I'm one of those. "Can I start y'all off with somethin' to drink?" she asked, pulling a pen out of her large hair. I found that to be particularly disturbing. However, she *did* pull a small pad of paper from her apron pocket.

"Water, please," Dad said. He was on this eternal diet that never seemed to show any results.

"I'll take a sweet tea. If y'all can, go ahead and throw a couple of them lemon slices in there, too," Mom said.

"Sure thing, sugar," our waitress said. "And for you?" She looked at me. "I can see it's your big night! My grandbaby just graduated this year, too. Do ya know Walter Ernesto?"

Goddamn the cap and gown to the lowest pits of hell. He probably didn't even go to school with me a day in his life. I acted like I was thinking to go along with it. I shook my head then ordered. "Uh, I'll have a beer, thanks." My dad cleared his throat and my mom looked like she was gonna pass out right there on the floor. The waitress just laughed a little. They didn't even serve beer there. "I'm kidding. I'll have chocolate milk, please." Judge, if you will, but chocolate milk is the king of dairy beverages. It's a helluva good drink. (For the record, I've never had much alcohol.)

"All righty. I'll be back in a few."

My parents began talking to each other about all of my scholarship possibilities. That was all they ever talked about anymore. My mom never had the chance to go to college. She said that she wanted me to marry "one of them smart lawyer girls", which I didn't care much about. I mean, yeah a smart girl would be nice, but not a lawyer. That was a terrible idea, if I ever heard one. If we got in a fight (which, knowing me, we often would) she would always win with an argument that was better executed than mine could ever be. And getting married was the last thing on my mind.

Just then, the entire restaurant grew ten times louder. A group of kids from my (former) school walked in with their parents. The guys were all hootin' and hollerin' "Freedom, babes, and beer!" while the girls just rolled their eyes. Hell, I'm a guy and I rolled mine, too. None of them, however, were wearing their cap and gown. I wanted to throw up the food I hadn't eaten yet. I looked like a total idiot. The proud, overzealous type.

"Yo! Waddup, Wade?" My cap was suddenly removed from my person by someone other than myself, which I guess was a good thing.

"Hey, Luke. What's up, man?" I said. He was one of my two close friends. (Saying "best friends" just seems kinda girly to me.)

"Not a lot for once. Nothin' but being free, son."

"Liking the feeling of graduation, I see."

"You know it. This shit is awesome. Never again will I have to step into the hell which is Hollow High. Jesus Christ, someone could get totally high feeling this way." I only agreed with part of that. The other part was illogical. "Hey, have you seen Bryce?" he asked.

"Uh, no I haven't. He didn't come in with y'all?" I couldn't help but say *y'all*. It's kind of branded in my DNA. I realized that I would have to refine my speech a bit for Harvard, though.

"Nope. He'll probably be here sooner or later. There's actually a waiting list for fuckin' Denny's. We made it just in time. If he doesn't show up, I bet ya he's making a batch of celebratory shine and tasting way too much of it. Anyway, I'm gonna go find my parents. I'm kinda starving."

"All right. Later," I said. Luke walked off, cheering again.

I imagine the loud obnoxious graduates were a thing that everyone got used to, because nobody seemed to mind it.

The waitress finally came back with our drinks. I took a long pull of my milk. It was already half empty. (I've never really been the optimistic type.) "Y'all ready to order?" The three of us nodded. She took my order first.

"I'll have a cheese burger. No cheese. Extra ketchup. And I wanna swap

14

the fries for onion rings. Thank you."

She looked confused. "So, ya just want a hamburger?"

"No, ma'am. I believe that they do not, or at least *should* not contain ham. People should technically call them beef burgers. It doesn't take a genius to figure that out." I couldn't help but laugh a little at my own private joke, considering the fact that I was a genius. "So, cheese burger. No cheese."

"Okay, then. That's different. Any sauce for your onion rings?"

"No, thanks."

She finished writing down my order. I guarantee she wrote hamburger with extra ketchup. I cringed at the thought. I wouldn't say that I'm picky. Just proper. "And what would you like?" she asked my mom, probably hoping her order would be normal and that we weren't just a family of weirdoes in some food cult or something.

"The country fried steak meal, please. And for my two sides, I'll take the mashed taters and green beans."

"One of my favorites," the waitress said. I really wish she were wearing a nametag. "And you, sir?"

"I'll just have the grilled chicken salad. Low-fat ranch on the side, please. Thanks."

"That's my man," Mom said. "You'll get them abs if you keep that up, baby." Gross.

"Okay, I'll put your orders in. I'll be right back with another chocolate milk, too." She smiled at me. She was missing several teeth. I smiled back.

I downed my fourth chocolate milk and scraped the extra ketchup off my plate with my last onion ring. My dad ate half of his salad and claimed to be full. I'm sure that he'd sneak off to buy a couple Snickers at the gas station when Mom fell asleep. She took sleeping pills, so when she was out, nothing, not even the apocalypse, could wake her up for at least eight hours.
Mom ate all her food and then ordered dessert. I have no idea where she kept it all. She wasn't even that big or anything. Don't get me wrong, she wasn't thin. But god she ate a lot. "Lord, am I full," she said. Hallelujah!

"Yeah, me, too," I said. I probably drank more than I actually ate. I really need to fill out one of these days. I'm still in that awkwardly tall and skinny stage of life that I assumed I would outgrow when I was twelve. Guys don't wanna be skinny. We wanna be buff! Or maybe that's stereotypical in the way that all girls want big...areas. Probably.

Dad leaned back in his chair and patted his stomach. "Sure did hit the spot." Lies. "I have to meet with the school board early tomorrow and find out my tutoring schedule. We should get home so I can hit the ol' sack." More lies. (And who the hell says "hit the ol' sack?") He just wanted to get the pills in Mom so she'd fall asleep and he could get some candy or a hotdog or

whatever he secretly eats like some teenage bulimic (without the puking part). He pulled out his wallet and left a seven dollar tip. I shouted a quick word of farewell to Luke and we were off.

Home wasn't particularly glamorous. Although we weren't poor, my parents decided to root themselves in this small trailer park in these God-forsaken woods that consisted of like a million creepy organisms that were probably deadly in some way and seven mobile homes. Only two of which were actually inhabited. It was a painfully boring way to live, but considering that my only two friends were guys that lack brain cells that aren't holding on to life with every ounce of their being, perhaps I am a painfully boring person. They probably couldn't tell either way.

In country songs (which I don't listen to, but are impossible to avoid in West Virginia), there's supposed to be a ton of unmarried sex, drugs, booze, and honkey-tonking going on in the trailer parks of southern America! Where the hell is all that fun!? (Not that I find any of those things to be fun.) The other trailer contains the lives of Edna and Gabe McElroy. They are lives with numbered days. They have been elderly for quite some time now. They were born that way as far as I know.

Every single year my parents made me formally invite them to Thanksgiving dinner. And every single year they always accept and offer to bring a pecan pie, sweet potato casserole, and creamed corn. Those elderlies are pretty good cooks. Better than the rotisserie chicken and instant mashed potatoes my mom tries to pass off as a homemade

Thanksgiving meal. It's not *bad.* It's just not good. The Indians and Pilgrims probably ate better than we did. For that reason, I was grateful for our quiet and somewhat grumpy neighbors. They made Thanksgiving, well, Thanksgiving.

*   *   *

I was lying in bed reading this book about how circles are nothing but edgeless, bloated triangles when I finally heard my mom's snoring. It sounded like all the loudness of the Indianapolis 500 my dad and I went to once. So, I waited. Sure enough, I heard the sneaky, yet still clumsy, sound of my dad's steps. It'd take him a good two minutes to make it to the family room. I thought I would have some fun. I took my house key from my nightstand, climbed out of the bedroom window, and ran to the front door. By the time I heard his slippers slide against the hardwood floor, I was already seated in his La-Z-Boy. "Hey, Dad." I laughed so hard. He actually took off one of his slippers and threw it at my face. I think he screamed a little, too.

"What the hell, Wade? What are you still doin' up?"

"Oh, nothing. If you don't mind, pick me up a bag of Skittles while you're out. Thank you." I was back in bed and reading about the true identity of shapes before his confused brain could create a logical response to what just happened.

CHAPTER TWO

The following morning I found a bag of Skittles in the cabinet on top of my favorite cereal: Cheerios. I smiled and slipped them into my pajama pant pocket. I measured out an exact serving of cereal and milk and finished eating within my average time of five minutes and thirty-two seconds. Then I got dressed and played a couple of games of chess online. My opponent was this kid from Japan who claimed to be nineteen. His ChessQuest profile picture showed someone who couldn't be any older than thirteen. Like, if you're gonna lie about your age, find a picture of some old Japanese guy. Not that hard to do. I don't know why he lied in the first place because he was pretty good. If he beat me at his real age, it would have been impressive. But he decided to lie. I had this headset where I could hear him and talk to him while we played if he had a similar device. He did.

Me: What's your name?

Random Japanese Liar: Hyako. The name of my father and his father and his father. What is your name?

I knew it was going to get interesting at that point.

Me: Wade Larson. The name of a soldier who did some pretty sick shit.

Hyako: Ha! Yes. Wade Hampton. I do know my history.

Dammit, I thought.

Hyako: Well, Wade, I do plan on destroying your American ass.

Me: We'll see about that, Hyako.

I spent the next three hours or so planning each move of my kings, knights, and pawns. I wasn't about to lose to some punk kid. I wasn't mentally prepared for such a loss. God, why was I nervous? I had done that exact same thing practically every single day since I was nine.

Hyako: You're being very quiet, Mr. Larson. You worried?"

Me: Not at all.

I checkmated him like there was no tomorrow. I won the first game.

Hyako: Fuck!

What a bad sport he was.

Me: Would your mother want you to curse like that?

Hyako: My mother doesn't give a *fuck* about what I do. Luckily for her, I'm not a sex addict, but if I were, I could be spending my days watching Russian porn and she *still wouldn't care!* Now, are you going to preach at me or are we going to fight like men?

This kid was serious. The next game was a draw and I noticed my sudden hunger. I decided to take advantage of my human needs. (That almost sounded dirty.) I put a finger over the tiny microphone in my headset. "MOM!" I yelled.

She ran into my room in her bra and jean shorts. I threw up a little in my mouth. "Christ, Wade. What?"

"Sorry, Mama."

She smiled, as I expected. She needed a new weakness. But her weakness was my strength. "It's okay, baby. What did you need?"

"Could you grab me, like, twelve Doritos?" I didn't know what the actual serving size was. YOLO.

"Sure thing."

"Thanks." She came back (this time with a shirt) holding a baggie containing twelve orange sodium-coated tortilla chips. She kissed my cheek and left, closing the door behind her.

Me: I have returned, Hyako.

Hyako: It's about time, mommy's boy. You're such a faggot. Now come on. It's your move.

I was almost amazed by how rude he was. I thought East Asians were supposed to be respectful. Either that was a lie, or his whole online persona was fictitious. Hard telling these days. I didn't really know any other Asian dudes I could compare him to. Actually, there was a Hawaiian guy in my trig class. I didn't know his name, though. I heard someone say that he flew back to Hawaii in a helicopter that his private pilot flew. That seemed unlikely.

Me: Someone's getting defensive, huh?

I circled the computer mouse over the board and moved my pawn. I heard his diabolical laughter.

Hyako: Oh, I am purely offensive at the moment, my friend.

His king jumped my knight. I knew that move was coming. Amateur.

Me: I'm getting a little hungry, man. Gonna grab a snack.

I shoved two chips into my mouth and chomped as loudly as I could into the mic.

Me: That's better.
My mouth was full. My dad would have given me a mini-lecture on manners. Several chunks flew across my desk. Hyako completely flipped out. It was kinda great.

Hyako: Ew! That's so fucking disgusting.

If he could have seen me, he would have vomited whatever Japanese people eat. Like, seaweed and shark fin burritos. Or sushi rolls. I double-jumped one of each of his pawns and knights.

Me: What? I can't hear you. TOO CRUNCHY!

Hyako: You're such a baby.

He was not good at being offensive in any way.

Hyako: I bet you're a forty-something fat ass in your mom's basement.

He was so wrong.

Me: Nope. Sorry to disappoint you. Now make your move.

I ate another Dorito.

Hyako: Ugh! I quit.

Thank God. He finally logged off. I know what you're thinking. I'm a pansy cheater afraid of losing to some foreign kid who may even be smarter than me. And to that I say: Ha! He was just So. Freaking. Annoying. That game could have lasted forever. I would have won, but I couldn't deal with any more of his sissy shit. I'm sure he went on to challenge someone much kinder than I.

My brain was sore. I needed to keep it well-maintained, so I finished the remaining nine chips, shutdown my computer, and went to bed. Maybe sleeping during the day as an unemployed person was a loserish thing to do, but it was Saturday, I had finally and thank-the-Lord graduated, and I intended to bask in the splendor of the moments before college. My phone buzzed twenty-nine seconds later. Then again seven seconds after that. (I count the ticks of my clock when I can't sleep. Much better than sheep.) The first was a text from Luke:

Dude. YES! Meet us at Pizza Hut. Clayton.

The second buzz was a text from Bryce:

God, I can't believe this shit actually worked!!! PH? I'm on my way this very second & my trunk is loaded with shine.

Both texts were confusing, but Bryce's just concerned me. Either "this shit" was some new drug he was on, or he and Luke planned something without involving me or my sage words of advice. Probably because I would have mentally accomplished the plan and explained all the ways it could and would fail. As much as their planning scared me, I didn't want to picture Bryce driving down mountainous highways high as fuck on some recently-discovered drug with a trunk filled with very flammable moonshine. I texted both of them back with the same message:

Okay? On my way. I'll bring you guys some Skittles.

(They both loved those little candies of lies.) I brushed my teeth, flossed, and brushed them again. Dad may or may not have been meeting with the school board, so the van was gone. But Mom had this crappy station wagon she hardly drove anywhere. I hated driving it, but

I suppose it got the job done. She was at the dinner table laughing to the point of tears at the funnies in the paper. "Sorry to interrupt, Mom."

She breathed deeply, in and out. It was a bit wheezy. "Oh, hey. I didn't see ya there. Gosh dang, you really gotta read these."

My IQ dropped fifty points just thinking about it. I found nothing about the comics to be the least bit amusing. Not enough intellectual stimulation to be entertaining. "Maybe later when I have the time. I'm busy with last minute college papers. But Luke and Bryce just texted me, probably about school. Mind if I use the car?"

"Sure. Where you goin' to?" I wanted to cry every time she ended a sentence with a preposition.

"Just over to Clayton."

"All right. Have fun. Stay out as long as you need to, since you're a man now and what have you." She kept calling me a man and variations of *her* man, which made me uncomfortable since that's what she always called my dad.

"Thanks. I'll see you later, Mom." There was another bout of laughter before I even made it out of the kitchen. They were not that funny! Jesus Christ.

We didn't have a garage because people who live in trailers generally aren't supposed to have nice cars. And my parents definitely did not. Even if we did have, like, a Ferrari or something, nobody ever drives through the area of forest where I lived. It was about as isolated as anyone could get in West Virginia.

My parents had a decent amount of savings, mostly because Dad had a decent job. Mom made quite a bit of money off tips at the bar, too. They just chose to live like a family of middle-class farmers struggling for financial survival in the Great Depression. But at least they provided me with Internet, a computer that wasn't ancient, and enough money to buy a few books a month, because I went through books like celebrities go through marriages. Way too many to keep track of.

I don't believe in libraries. Well, I believe they are good and should exist and that Carnegie is pretty cool for funding them even in death, but I don't like to use them. I cannot (literally) read a book without underlining, highlighting, or writing analytical notes in the margins. I once forgot the book I was reading was not technically mine, so I treated it as if it were. When I finished, I noticed the library seal on the inside cover and I was like, "SHIT!" I turned it in the day it was due like everything was fine and dandy. The librarian called me three hours later and made me pay to replace it. It was one of those hardback non-fiction books that just so happened to be, like, thirty bucks. At least she let me keep the copy she said I "defaced."

Anyway, I drove the old station wagon that I swore would combust every time I ran over a pebble down the dirt lane that transitioned to gravel (a road of many pebbles) until it finally merged with the highway. I tuned the radio to some station that *actually played The Mountain Goats.* After my ears were permanently damaged by a couple shitty songs, there was success in the form of John Darnielle's genius. I drove the last ten minutes in silence. Well, there was the frequent honking of semi-trucks and the whistling of trains hauling coal to factories for purification—the cells that flowed in the veins that gave life to the ebbing heart of Mountain Hollow. I've learned to ignore those things. Seventeen years of practice.

When I got to Pizza Hut, the parking lot was empty except for a couple delivery cars. Luke and Bryce always parked in the alley behind the restaurant since there was never any traffic. Anyone could do anything illegal back there without getting caught. Or if you were stupid enough to get caught, most people in my neck of the woods were too drunk or wasted on crystal meth to turn you in. That included much of the police.

Bryce had his trunk popped open, revealing at least thirty mason jars of shine. I have no idea how he made it, but he always had five crates of it at any given time. I guess he knows some guys who know some guys who will buy it for five dollars a jar. I've never tried it. The smell alone burns my nose like turpentine or my mom's nail polish remover. I'm afraid of what it would do to my organs. Bryce seemed to manage well. Luke's taken a few sips every now and then, but that's all. All he does is smoke, and he's been doing that since he was twelve. Not even anything hard like cocaine. Just cigarettes. He stole two cigars from his dad a few years ago. They were supposed to taste like cinnamon, so I took a puff. It did not taste like cinnamon. It tasted like a house burning down in my mouth. I don't really wanna talk about that experience. Let's just say it was bad. I just told myself that was one less pressure I would have to worry about when I went to college. Anyway, his dad found out because they turned out to be the super expensive kind from Cuba or Guam or maybe somewhere in South America. He had every right to be mad at us, but why would anyone in their right mind pay a large sum of money to torment your poor lungs? They just try their hardest to serve us long and well until we die.

Luke and Bryce heard me pull up. They put out their cigarettes and screwed on the lids of their jars. "Got your messages," I said.

Bryce laughed and his words were only slightly slurred when he said, "Yes, sir, ya did." He stumbled through the back entrance that was clearly marked EMPLOYEES ONLY. Nobody listened to it, though. Luke followed and grinned in a way that made me uncomfortable, like watching a scary movie about demons that suck the souls out of innocent puppies for no reason at all but to be cruel to puppies. I was genuinely afraid, and it took a lot to scare me. There was something terrifying about any plan that those two could have arranged. I slammed down Bryce's trunk before walking inside. He would have been pissed off if somebody stole so much as a sip of his moonshine.

CHAPTER THREE

We ordered two large pepperoni pizzas and two sides of breadsticks. We were on our third pitcher of Pepsi. Luke tried to order us a few bottles of beer. He called our waitress a "sexy little thang", hoping that would get her to serve it to us, but she actually seemed to have a few standards. Not a common thing where I'm from.

I ate two slices and four breadsticks then let them have the rest. I don't actually like pepperoni, but I wasn't the one paying. I picked it off and let them fight over the extra greasy circles of processed meat byproduct, or whatever it was. I'm not a psycho health fanatic or anything. I'd just rather not die before the age of twenty-five. Psycho health fanatics wouldn't even eat pizza. "So, are you going to tell me why the three of us are here eating decent food without an apparent reason to celebrate?"

"Did you bring the Skittles?" Bryce asked. I tossed the bag onto the table. Bryce poured half the bag in Luke's hand and then finished off the other half himself.

"Tell me again why you refuse to eat good things," Luke said, and shoved his handful of candy into his mouth. He chased it down with a chug of Pepsi and the pepperoni off my plate.

"I don't refuse to eat good things. Bryce, what's the motto of Skittles?"

"'Taste the rainbow,'" he said.

"Correct. Rainbows contain red, orange, yellow, green, blue, indigo, and violet. The traditional bag does not include all of those. They only have blue in the specialty flavors and indigo and violet do not exist at all! That's their first error. Second, one cannot taste a rainbow. If I found a leprechaun who tried his hardest to lead me to a rainbow, we would never be able to physically reach it, even with badass magical powers. It's nothing but a trick of the atmosphere." I heard Luke and Bryce laugh a little. "If you can't find it, how in the hell can a company tell you what it tastes like in a candy that more or less resembles unicorn poop? The advertisement is completely false. *You* are the victims. *I* am the wise consumer."

"You take shit way too seriously, dude," Bryce said. "Just eat the motherfucking candy."

"I can't. You guys already ate it all."

"They go buy some. They're like, less than a dollar," Luke suggested. Because I so didn't know that.

"No, thanks. I had my dad buy those last night because I needed to prove a point about his private habits."

"Like, your dad eats Skittles when he gets himself off?" Bryce asked. I groaned and rolled my eyes. *Of course* he would think I was implying that.

"Jesus fucking Christ! That's not was I was saying. His private *eating* habits. Better?"

"HA HA HA! That sounds so much worse."

"Fuck you, Bryce."

"Whatever, man," Luke said. "We didn't bring you here to talk about any of your dad's habits, sexual or otherwise."

Not even my best friends were capable of understanding me. "So, what's going on?" I looked at Bryce. "What shit worked? You guys aren't on some weird drug trend, are you?"

Luke was the one to explain. "Drugs? What? No clue what gave you that idea." He acted like that would be out of character for them. "So, here's the deal. In March, me and Bryce applied for the University of California. Today, we both got our acceptance letters in the mail." I was shocked to hear this. You have no idea.

"Dude, that's awesome!" And I was not being sarcastic. I was happy for them. I thought it was great that even they were getting a shot at having an actual future. "At least you'll both know somebody there. Maybe you can share a dorm if you request it early enough."

Luke continued. "The thing is, we're not going."

"Forgive my common sense and not knowing the answer, but then why did you apply?"

"Because we needed a believable excuse to go to Cali for a while. We are men. We like ladies. Tan ladies with long legs and bikinis that are just a bit too tight. What better place than California?"

"That is really stupid." They truly amazed me sometimes. Most of the time, if I were being honest.

"How? I think that it's rather brilliant."

"Won't your parents find out?"

"Nope. We may not be as smart as Mr. Wade Larson, but we aren't complete idiots." I disagreed, but kept quiet to give him his moment. "We're gonna pack our bags like we're leaving for college, cry with our mom's, man-hug our dads. Well, I will. Then we'll just take off in that direction. Bryce bought a GPS with some of his moonshine money. I pitched in a little."

I looked at Bryce. He was in his own little world, drinking soda from the pitcher. "This could be the worst idea I have ever heard in my entire life, except for, like, certain congressional tactics," I said.

"Yeah, I'm sure someone told Eddy the same thing when he invented the light bulb."

"Edison. Thomas Edison. Not Eddy. And, yes, I'm aware of that. I'm a fucking genius. What don't I know?"

"Conceited much?"

"Sorry. But seriously, quiz me."

Bryce laughed and slapped his hands on the table. "I got a question for ya, buddy."

"Um, okay?"

"Why do I love me some shine?" The drunkenness had finally set in completely.

Jesus, really? I thought. "Because you're inherently opposed to making good decisions."

"Sounds smart enough for me," he said with a mouthful of pizza. The sound he was producing with food in his mouth almost made me feel bad for Hyako. But not quite.

I changed the subject back to where we started. "Well, won't your parents want to see you graduate? Finishing college will be a huge deal."

"They ain't gonna waste a trip to California for that," Luke said.

"Then won't they expect you to have a diploma in four years?"

"We've thought of that, too." Well, wasn't he just prepared for everything? Almost as if he planned it logically. "So, we Googled fake diplomas, right? It's amazing what you can find. There's this guy in Alaska who makes fake IDs and such, as well as diplomas for any college. They're kinda not super expensive for what you're getting. It saves a ton in tuition costs. Like ten for community colleges, thirty for state universities, then like seventy-five for Ivy League schools...Like Harvard."

"And how do you plan on getting there?"

"To Alaska?"

"Yup."

"He ships anywhere."

"Ah." Then I suddenly noticed the emphasis he put on Harvard. "Wait wait wait. You *cannot* expect me to go with you. I refuse to take any part of this whatsoever."

"Aww, come on, man. Live a little and for once in your life stop giving a fuck so much," Bryce said. "I gotta piss."

"God, have some fucking class or I won't *GIVE A FUCK* when I kick you out," the waitress shouted at Bryce. Because, ya know, that was a very classy thing for a lady to do.

I dropped my voice to one of those whisper-yells that basically turned out to be the same number of decibels as casual conversation. "I am *not* skipping Harvard just to check out girls in California and get wasted all the time!"

"Why the hell not?"

"It's just not a good idea whatsoever. Do you plan on marrying some random girl just because she's hot, but potentially has the worst morals ever?"

"Since when do you care about morals?"

"I'm a virgin. You're not. Answer the question."

"You never went to prom. I did. And, no. I'm more of player for life, know what I mean? If I want some, I'll get some. But not with the same person forever. Marriage. Ugh. That just leads to an expensive ring, expensive ceremony, expensive honeymoon, and expensive divorce. Then you gotta factor in the possibility of child support. I'm broke. I mean, if I were to accidentally get drunk and knock some girl up while unprotected, I might marry her if she's not too bitchy. But only in that situation."

"You are such an ass, Luke."

"Yeah. I've been told." He sounded proud when he said it and it kind of pissed me off.

When all of us drove back home, we went to my house so Luke and Bryce could show me www.InsanelyRealDocuments.com. The website looked awful. If someone couldn't make a decent site, how in the hell could that someone forge decent diplomas? "Isn't this, like, extremely illegal?"

"Of course it is," Luke said.

"But it's not like we plan on using them to land some frickin' awesome job that pays a million a year for sitting at a CEO desk or operating on people's brains. We get them to show the folks, and that's about it," Bryce said. "It can't fail."

"Anything can fail provided there are undesirable and unexpected circumstances." I typed Harvard English Degree in the website's search bar and I beheld a photo that actually resembled my dad's diploma from Harvard that my mom kept on the refrigerator. She had it laminated, along with my birth certificate. "Wow. That looks really good."

"I know, right?" Luke said. "His web design skills suck like a mosquito, but you gotta admit he makes a mean fake document. Are you in, Wade?"

I hated myself for even starting to consider it. The whole thing was stupid. I knew it was. I was supposed to be the logic of the group. I sighed loudly. "I don't know. Harvard is my dream school. You know that. It may be the only chance I have to get out of this town and actually be somebody."

"Maybe nobody in this town is meant to matter," Bryce said. Those may have been the most thoughtful words I ever heard him say. "Besides, isn't Harvard just your dad's dream?"

I ignored his last question. "I refuse to accept that. The universe is full of people who are and were nobody. I will not accept that fate. I want to feel and experience and love the little and unknown parts of life. I want to be remembered when I am dead. One day, I will be nothing but dust in the earth. But I will never be just nothing."

"Well, maybe you'll matter to somebody, like some chick in Cali who's super hot but also has the same fetish for your depressing psychobabble shit," Luke said. "Your dad went to Harvard. Has he really done anything that makes him significant enough to be remembered in shitty textbooks fifty or a hundred years from now? You want to leave this place, but can you guarantee that will ever happen? Your dad is still stuck here. Living it up, I'm sure."

"No, but—"

"Exactly. Harvard is not a ticket to this perfect life you're looking for. What if this trip changes your life? What if mattering is more than being famous for something nobody else has ever done, even if you only matter to one person?"

Don't do it, Wade, I told myself. But I didn't listen. I told myself I did it just to get them to shut up, but I knew it wasn't true. Some part of me wanted the hope of something bigger. "I'll give you a semester's worth of time. That's all. If this turns out to be the worst decision of my life, I should be able to make up the work quickly. Then you guys can stay in California without me."

"Hell yes! Bryce, what did I tell you?"

"That Wade can be talked into doing anything if you make it sound good enough."

"That is not accurate information," I said.

"It's true," Luke said. "Remember that one time in seventh grade when I convinced you to steal the frogs from the science lab because—"

"Okay, you swore to Jesus that you would never bring that up again."

"I know, I know, but I just really needed to prove my point." Luke laughed. "That was such a beautiful moment, though."

I punched him in the arm. "Ow!" Luke rubbed where I hit.
"And one day you will learn to not mention that day."

*   *   *

Dinner was awkward that night. Not for Mom and Dad, because they were blissfully unaware of my youthful ignorance, but for me. "I'll bet you're gonna miss Mama's cookin', aren't ya, son?"

I swallowed a nervous lump in my throat. Actually, I think it was peas. "Yes, sir," I mumbled.

"Shucks, boys. Maybe I don't know how good a cook I am. Should I try out some new recipes? Loretta got me them nice cookbooks for Christmas a few years ago. They're just gatherin' dust." Loretta was the owner of the bar where she worked. The books were probably stolen from the library.

"No! I mean, everything you make now is just perfected so well already, darling," Dad said.

Nice save, I mouthed across the table. He nodded. "How was the food when you were at Harvard?" I asked. "Not sure if I can make it four years with only Ramen and peanut butter care packages from Mom. No offense."

"None taken, honey."

"The food wasn't bad, really. If the tradition is still going, Tuesday is pie day."

"Awesome." I tried to be enthusiastic, but I wasn't pulling it off well. "It was. The cafeteria chefs came in early and baked a couple dozen pies or so."

"Good to know, Dad. I'll have to try it and let you know how it is." My conversation sounded so generic and fake. I hated lying to them. I had to have been the most disappointing son ever. Then I remembered that Mussolini and Stalin had parents, too.

"You boys best quit talkin' now. Your steak is gonna get cold. And *you'd* better eat all your peas, then help yourself to seconds," she told Dad.

The steak was actually cold (and extremely similar to beef jerky) when she gave it to us, but nobody said anything. As long as we kept quiet, she didn't think there's anything wrong with it. She really did try her hardest, bless her heart.

Later that night, I heard Dad sneak out of his room again, and again I met him in his recliner. He sighed. "What do you want?"

"A hotdog and chocolate milk, please. Extra ketchup."

"Yeah, sure," he said. Now that I knew his secret, he'd give me anything I wanted because he knew I would tell Mom. She'd probably smack him in the face with a frying pan. And that's not a redneck metaphor for getting chewed out. Domestic peace was in my hands. That must have been how the United Nations feels every day—controlling and oddly threatening. Except they didn't get mediocre gas station food as a reward for their accomplishments.

CHAPTER FOUR

My letter from Harvard arrived two days later. I decided to sleep until noon, since I rarely had the opportunity to do so. My dad knocked on my bedroom door and walked in, my mom right behind him. I sat up, confused. My first reaction was to wonder if it my birthday? It was May twenty-ninth. I was pretty sure my birthday wasn't until August twenty-fourth, on which day I would finally be eighteen. I tried to remember if there were any weird foreign holidays, but my brain was too tired to do any immediate work. (I later realized that is was Ascension, the day forty days after Easter. But considering I don't find myself to be particularly religious, I didn't really need to know that.) "Uh, good morning?" I said.

My mom squealed like a teenage girl cutting class for a One Direction concert, but in a slightly lower octave. So, like a gay man at a One Direction concert. But I'm not calling my mom a gay man, I swear. "I can't wait anymore! Tell him, Ronnie!" she said. "We couldn't wait to open it, honey. Sorry about that, Wadey."

"Okay, okay. Calm down, babe. I'm just as excited as you are." It was kinda gross when they used their pet names in front of me. My dad's actual name is Robert. Something was always up when she called him Ronnie. My mom's name is Cathy, but he never used her name or any variations of it. She was usually just darling or honey or Mama. Babe was weird.

Dad unfolded a sheet of paper and began to read aloud. "Dear Mr. Larson," he said.

"No way…"

"We are pleased to inform you that your application has been processed and we are happy to welcome you to Harvard University."

"OH MY GOD ARE YOU KIDDING ME RIGHT NOW!?" I was excited even though I knew I wasn't going right away. I was good enough for Harvard, and in that moment, it was good enough for me. Seeing my mom and dad that happy made me feel happy, too (and a little shitty). They were an odd couple, but I believe they will always be madly in love.

"We are bein' one hundred percent for real!" Mom said. She ran and nearly squeezed the life out of me with that hug. I squeezed back. "I am so proud to be the mama of Wade Duke Larson." (My parents are big fans of the old Dukes of Hazzard stuff. My middle name is the unfortunate result of their fandom.)

"I love you, Mama."

"I love you more." She sounded so sincere and it broke my heart that I was lying to her. But I told myself that is was just temporary.
I think it's always the mothers who love parenthood the most. We kids give them nine months of hell and vomiting and weird sandwiches that contain that contain both pickles and peanut butter. Sometimes they don't even make it to see their baby one time. But they will always love

us more.

"I know," I whispered. I swear to God I almost cried.

Dad hugged me next, surprisingly. I could hardly remember the last time he hugged me like that. His big hands swallowed my shoulders when he grabbed them. Then he looked me in the eyes with the attention of a military officer and firmly shook my hand. "I knew you would make it, son. I knew you would. I am damn proud of you, Wade."

"Not without you. Thank you." I shook his hand back. I think he and I have only said that we love each other a few times, but neither of us had to. I always respected him and he respected me for it. In the sentence of our relationship that seems to be missing a valuable part of speech, love is the understood subject. It isn't clearly seen right away, but once you get through all the flowery adjectives and prepositions, you will never be able to not see it.

"You're welcome, Wade."

I tried to change the subject considering the fact that I felt guilty as hell. "Did you hear that Bryce and Luke were accepted by the University of California?"

"Oh, did they really?" Mom seemed happy enough. "Gosh, I almost feel like they're my sons as much as you are. Good for them. Smart boys." Nope. They were not smart at all. Luke wasn't as bad as Bryce was, though. I'll give him that. I don't think Dad really cared much. He probably tutored them in summer school at one point or another and saw how they behave.

"Yeah, we've all talked about it a little bit. I think we're going to leave on the same day, drive a while, grab a bite to eat somewhere, then finally head separate ways. Too bad California and Massachusetts have to be so far away, you know it?" I tried to feign sadness.

"That'll be fine, son," Dad said, though I'm sure he hated the idea. "I can't believe it. Harvard's actually runnin' in the family now. You'll have to convince your son to keep the line alive."

"Dad, I'm seventeen. I don't want to think about commitment to a girlfriend right now, let alone a permanent wife and kid. And I promise I'm not gonna be having a bunch of drunk sex in the dorms. Or sober sex, honestly. So you won't have to worry me there. That's a plus." That's actually how I happened. Mom worked in a crappy bar even then. Dad went to get drunk with a group of his irresponsible college friends. He flirted (or she did). He sneaked her on campus after her shift. You can figure out the rest. It's not something I like to think about in detail.

He chuckled. His mind was, no doubt, in the same time and place as mine. The difference was that mine was nostalgia I never really experienced. "Glad to
hear it. You've always been more mature than I was at your age."

"I don't know who I got it from." Which was true. "Must be my generation." Which was a lie. I thought of Luke and Bryce.

Dad handed me the envelope. "There's a couple final forms in there you need to fill out. Just send 'em in when you get a few minutes. Mama and I are going out for a little while later. Need anything?"

"Um, Mountain Dew?" I knew he hated when I drank that stuff, but I couldn't help that I liked it. Maybe even as much as chocolate milk. My tongue just doesn't enjoy, like, the juices of spinach and wheat grass or whatever.

I know he had to force out his answer. "Fine."

When they left a few hours later, I called Luke. Bryce was already at Luke's house to play some video game about shooting drug dealers in random major cities, so that was convenient. Luke picked up on the first ring. "What's up?" I heard Bryce in the background: Kill him kill him KILL HIM! Dude, he has, like, thirty zillion pounds of crack on his person. Just fucking shoot the nihilistic bastard!

"Having fun?" I asked.

"Hell yeah I am," Bryce said. Apparently I was on speaker. "You need to drop whatever faggoty, geniusy shit you're doing and come over and shoot some illegals with us. I don't care if you're comfortably in Spiderman footy pajamas talking to the president about creating Spiderman in a lab. It can wait."

"I haven't owned footy pajamas since I was, like, four. I'll pass you up on that. Maybe later. The world needs a superhero to be synthetically created right this very instant or else all humanity will be lost within the next twenty seconds." Sometimes when Bryce gets really stupid, you just have to go along with it. "I am literally sitting in the Situation Room right now."

"So, why'd you call?" Luke asked over the sound of Bryce's profanity, screams of animated characters, and gunfire. It was a rather unpleasant sound. That's why I preferred chess. It's quiet and relaxing.

"I got my letter from Harvard."

"No shit?"

"Shit."

"You smart son of a bitch! Awesome, bro. Now the plan is basically official, right?"

"Uh, yeah. Basically."

"Why do you not sound so ridiculously excited that you might throw up sparkling fairies?" Bryce asked.

"That doesn't even sound fun. Like, how did they get inside me to begin with? Anyway, I don't really know why I don't sound uber thrilled. Well, I kinda do. You guys should have seen my parents today. They were so happy for me. I feel like it's not fair to them. I feel really bad about this. I'm not doing it happily, just so you guys know."

"Does a parent really want anything more than they want their children to be consumed with the purest of blisses?" I could not believe that

Bryce said that.

"That sounds too similar to Enlightenment. I don't think either I or my parents are Buddhists." *Game over,* a manufactured female voice said.

"Look, you're getting me killed, Wade," Luke said. "If you are going to sit around sulking about your potentially and likely bad decisions, don't call me to do it."

"I'm not sulking. I'm doubting."

"Same thing."

"Not really. Sulking is to—"

"Do not go all Merriam-Webster on me. I swear to Jesus."

"Sorry." I only had two friends in the entire universe. Even they were annoyed by my nerdish ways. It wasn't like I could fucking help it.

"Do you wanna come over or not? I don't care what you do. I'd rather you did. We ordered a lot of Chinese. Like enough food in noodles alone to feed a small to medium Asian village. My mom's drunk and passed out on the couch downstairs, and my dad is doing, you know…" Luke trailed off.

"The usual?"

"The usual." (The usual being watching reruns of old soaps.) I wish I were kidding.

"Ah."

"I'm not proud. I'm really not."

"Yeah. Life just sucks sometimes. But as long as life doesn't make you suck, too, it's okay. You gotta fight the suck. Anyway, I'll get to bed early tonight. I'd like to savor my last moment of life."

"You're such a pussy. God, your life hasn't even started yet. Neither have mine or Bryce's. He and I are just honest about it. You will live an entire lifetime on this trip. I promise you."

"You'd better be right."

CHAPTER FIVE

After ending the phone call, my mind imagined every way the trip could go wrong. Bryce could get drunk and wreck the van off a mountain while Luke and I slept. Harvard administrators would probably call my parents to ask why I wasn't attending any of my classes. My mom would send me a quadrillion care packages of Ramen and cookies and juice and call me repeatedly to ask why I haven't thanked her. Eventually they would be returned to her doorstep since nobody was there to pick them up. My dad would probably start freaking out and send an entire squadron of police helicopters to search for my decaying body of flesh in a field somewhere. There was no way I could get away with it. I was the only one who *actually couldn't.*

Luke's life was sad. Bryce's was worse, which is one of the reasons I learned to put up with his bullshit. His parents were put in jail indefinitely about four years ago for robbing a Subway restaurant. They took fifty dollars and a dozen chocolate chip cookies at gunpoint. The bail was, well, let's just say a lot. Were it not for the gun, the charges would have been much less severe. They're beyond poor, so they'll be in there a while. They probably still are as far as I know. I think that's why Bryce started moonshining. He knew he'd make a lot of money, and he did. But it's not for his parents anymore. Then he just made it to pay the bills and keep the house and get drunk a lot. He stopped giving a fuck a long time ago. He visited his mom and dad every now and then, because he felt like it was his obligation as their son, but that doesn't mean he gave a fuck at all.

On the other hand, my life is completely normal and boring and contained two relatively involved parents who genuinely cared about my personal well-being. I knew that if pulled the whole trip off by some God-given miracle, it would deservedly make me (unofficially, of course) the most sneakily awesome person to ever live.

Mom and Dad came back home around three o' clock in the morning. I heard the clicks of my mom's high heels on my bedroom floor. I covered up in my comforter and pretended to be asleep. She kissed my cheek. *Does she always do this?* I wondered. She whispered goodnight to me and then I heard her walk away. My bedroom door creaked shut. When I knew she was gone, I rolled over to find a bottle of Mountain Dew on my nightstand. I twisted the cap, took a few drinks in spite of having already brushed my teeth, held it in my mouth for a few seconds, and swallowed. I repeated until the caffeinated contents of the bottle were gone. It took 279 ticks of the clock. It took another 836 ticks for me to fall asleep.

I woke up at six o'clock in the morning exactly and weighed the pros and cons of not going to college.

Pros:
Adventure.
Thrills.

Possibly becoming a person who isn't actually afraid to do abnormal things such as skateboarding down Mount Everest during avalanche season.

Cons:
Misfortune.
Illegal happenings.
Forever being stuck as a coalminer.

While a future as a coalminer did seem like a big boulder of suck waiting to crush an innocent bystander, who didn't want people to walk up to them and say, "Hey, weren't you that guy who skated down that mountain?" Nobody walked up to you to ask, "Hey, aren't you that coalminer guy?" Don't get me wrong. Coal is super fantastic for, like, the economic stability of Mountain Hollow and pretty much all of West Virginia, but I wanted nothing more than to have that not be my future. The mere thought of it was suffocating.

I called Luke again. He was usually up kinda early for reasons I will never know.

"Hello?" he said and yawned.

"Did I wake you up?"

"Nope. I never actually went to bed. Bryce is still here. He's asleep in the bathtub I think. If he puked in there, I am so making him clean it up." He sounded tired and deadpan.

"Did he get into your mom's beer fridge?" It's happened many times before, too. If there was alcohol anywhere within his general radius, he would find it.

"Unfortunately, but you know what the fucked up thing is? She doesn't even care! I'm kinda thinking that she could be one of his shine customers. What kind of shit is that? She said, and I quote, 'I respect a fellow drinker in need.' Christ. What the hell is wrong with the frickin' world?"

"Everything," I said, thinking about my decision and how in a sane world, I would never have made that particular decision. Everything was wrong the goddamn world. "I'm gonna go."

"Wait, what?"

"I'll go with you and Bryce. I don't wanna be the coalminer. I wanna be the extreme skateboarder. 'Life's for the living, so live it, or you're better off dead.'"

"Umm? I'm confused."

"It's a line from one of my favorite songs. I'm sure I've played it for you…Never mind. Just a metaphor I was using to weigh the pros and cons of going with you."

"If I were a quarter as smart as you, life could be all right." He laughed.

"You act like life is alright to me." Really. He never let a thing in the world bother him. I was maybe even a little jealous.

"Key word: act. Maybe I have a career in those hideously cheap indie movies.

"Perhaps. The credits will list you as Nonchalant Person # 4."

"Yes! Dude, I'm feeling that. I can totally feel the fan base forming." Bryce walked in Luke's room. "Uh, hang on a sec. Bryce is alive."

"I feel like I deposited all of my organs and all of my dignity in your tub last night. Or this morning. I don't really remember either way. I just feel empty and dizzy and weird and hungry," I heard Bryce say.

"Then do the world a favor and go clean up your organs and dignity. The mop is in the kitchen closet. There should be a bucket and some bleach in there, too. Have at it. Use hot water," Luke said.

"Fuck you, Luke. Makin' a sick man clean up the motherfucking product of his sickness."

"You're not sick! You drank my mom's booze and got drunker than a slutfucker." I wanted to ask what exactly a slutfucker was, but I was kinda content not knowing that one particular thing. I mean, a slut was someone who fucks a lot. So, was Luke calling Bryce a fucker who fucks people who fuck a lot? I don't know. It was too many fucks to give. I assumed Luke was talking to me now. "Sorry about that. I told you I'd make him clean it up. Last time, I tried to be nice and clean it up, but I threw up right on top of his puke. My mom cleaned it up. But she'll never do it again."

"Now I know not to go to your house and get drunk with your mom's private alcohol stash."

"Sometimes it's not always best to learn from experience."

"I agree."

"So, why'd you call me again? I forgot." I suppose our conversation had taken some odd turns.

"To tell you that I'm going with you guys. For sure this time. No doubts."

"Oh, yeah. Bryce is so gonna flip when I tell him."

"If he lives that long. You should probably check on him. I've never ingested either moonshine or bleach, but I could imagine them tasting similar enough to where he wouldn't care. That would probably kill him slowly and painfully."

"Good idea, Wade. You're probably right."

"I'm always right. Haven't you learned that by now?"

"No, because it isn't true. You are wrong about the perfection that is Skittles and pepperoni."

"Whatever. I'm gonna go read something."

"You are so sad. You desperately need this trip." He hung up the phone.

I walked over to my bookshelf and chose a random book. When I turned on the light in my bedroom, I noticed that it was a biography of John Peake Knight. He's the guy who invented traffic lights.

I fell back asleep halfway into the first chapter. He was not a particularly interesting person.

CHAPTER SIX
&
THREE MONTHS LATER

I may be an intelligent person, but I am not good with planning and organization. I had just realized it was August fourteenth and I needed to leave on the fifteenth. I set my alarm for the ungodly hour of midnight and prayed to the God I wasn't sure I believed in to let that be enough time to pack. I grabbed a small suitcase and a large duffel bag from my closet. Both were dusty, so I sneezed about nineteen times in a row. They were a Christmas gift from my parents a few years ago. We never traveled, so I never knew why they bought them for me in the first place, but they came in handy now. I wasn't fond of the pattern, though. It was like some kind of paisley design that most grandmothers wear as shirts.

I unzipped the suitcase and tossed in about a week's worth of socks and boxers, two pairs of shorts, four pairs of jeans, and five random shirts that were mostly just polos. That was a good time to be unfortunately so skinny, since small clothes did take up much less space. I didn't bother to fold anything but the shirts. You can get away with wrinkly pants, but never wrinkly shirts. Then you just look like a poor person who can't afford an iron or an unprofessional one who doesn't care. That's what Dad always used to tell me, anyway.

I quickly brushed my teeth and flossed and gargled with mouthwash before also tossing them into the suitcase. I had exactly seventy-three dollars and nine cents saved up, so I put my wallet with my money and driver's license in there, too. I'd be kinda screwed if I forgot that. I had no idea how Luke and Bryce planned on our survival for the next unknown number of months. I knew that my money would hardly last me a day in the real world, let alone provide for three. I ate two bowls of cheerios in case it happened to be my last meal.

I checked the time on our old microwave, which I'm kinda certain was the first model ever invented. It was only 1:09. I guess midnight was more than enough time after all. So I took a shower. Probably the last shower I was going to have in a scarily long time.

I let the water fall down the muscles and skin of my back, gradually increasing the heat until it was at the highest possible temperature. I stood there like that until I felt it start to cool down. I rinsed the shampoo from my hair and turned off the water. I walked around the house naked because my parents were asleep and because I fucking could. I ate a third bowl of Cheerios just to finish off the box so it wouldn't grow sadly stale without my being there to eat it. My mom only ate Fruit Loops, which was sort of unfair to dad. She made him eat this Kashi stuff that looked strikingly similar to the food I used to feed my hamster, Yeti, in third grade. But then he died and I never had another pet after that. I was very happy to not be him. Dad, I mean, not Yeti. Though I wouldn't want to be a hamster either.

After eating again, I went back to my room to pack as many books as I could. The difficult part was actually choosing my favorites. I estimated that twenty books could fit easily in the duffel bag. I know it's weird and probably a waste of money and kind of unnecessary, but I owned every single one of my books in both hardback and paperback. I will explain. Hardback books are just classy to own. They're more expensive, but really nice to have. Paperbacks are good for travel. Every time I went to Wal-Mart with my mom, I would bring a book and read while she shopped. I have never ran into anything or anybody. Also, they weigh a lot less and if they're damaged, I won't have a potentially literal and fatal heart attack. I chose a few of the essentials like *Pride and Prejudice* (yes, I actually like it. It's a classic. Not a girl book), *To Kill a Mockingbird,* and the entire *Harry Potter* series. I added a couple random math books (including the one about the circles really being triangles) even though I'm kinda bad at math, a dictionary, a history book, *Slaughterhouse Five,* several pens and notebooks, and a Walkman that plays CDs because I'm old-school cool. (Which is probably a very uncool thing to say.) I don't ever really download MP3s or whatever. They make YouTube for that. If I've heard enough decent singles by an artist, then I consider buying the album. Finally, I managed to squeeze in my favorite board game, travel Scrabble.

I hauled my luggage into the living room and checked the time on my phone: 4:57. I groaned. I didn't know why I was being so impatient. It wasn't like I was looking forward to living a life of lies or anything. To pass the time, I went back to my room again to play a couple games of online chess. Though most of the Americans on ChessQuest were probably asleep, foreigners were wide awake and I was ready to go. Thankfully, it wasn't a Japanese douchebag. That time I was paired with this fourteen-year-old kid from South Africa named Robbie. "Isn't it kinda early there?" he asked me.

"Uh, yeah. So early it's gross," I said.

"Do you play chess when you can't sleep?"

I laughed. "No, I just woke up stupidly early. I'm supposed to be leaving for college today, but my moronic friends convinced me not to go to college and take a road trip with them instead. I'm probably not a good influence, so I don't suggest that you ever do that."

"Sounds really fun! School sucks. Like, everybody thinks I'm gay, so I have no friends."

"Are you? If you were and people didn't like you for that, you need to find better friends."

"No! That's the thing that bothers me. I'm totally straight. I don't have anything against gay people. I think my cousin is gay. Anyway, my school is just a bunch of freaking homophobes. Nobody likes me as their friend, and all the girls think I'm gay. I just wanna, like, go on a hypothetical killing spree."

Wow. That kid had it rough. "Just tell them to piss off."

"I tried. They turned me into the counselor who tried to convince me that it's okay to open up about my sexuality. Now the school makes me talk to him twice a week. I hate it, because there's never anything to talk about. I don't need to talk to anyone about anything."

"That really sucks."

"Tell me about it." He sighed. "But whatever. Just a few more years."

We went on like that for a couple hours. There was more conversation than actual playing, but I didn't mind. He seemed like a really smart kid. He almost reminded me of me at that age...Oh, God. No no no no no. I'm too young to look back at my youth like that.

It was finally a little after seven. Mom and Dad came in the living room to find me reading in Dad's recliner. "Oh, hey," I said, acting like I wasn't expecting them. I stood.

"Are you all packed?" Mom asked.

"Yeah. Got it all ready last night. I feel like I'm forgetting something, but everybody feels that way when they pack, even if they triple check." That was just an assumption, since I had never packed for anything important and long-term.

She laughed. "Ya got that right."

"When are you taking off?" Dad asked. I know he didn't like either of my friends.

"I was about to head out soon. Just wanted to say bye to you and Mama first."

Mom hugged me. "Well, we don't want ya to be late. You've got such a long drive ahead of you."

I hugged her back, which was always awkward. I'm nearly a foot taller than she is. "Yeah. I got plenty of sleep, so you don't have to worry about that." I picked up my bags.

"Let me carry those for you," Dad said.

"Thanks."

I popped the trunk of the station wagon and Dad tossed my luggage inside. He handed me a thick envelope. "It has a couple hundred dollars in it. That should cover most of your gas. I filled up the tank last night, too." My dad smacked the side of the car. "She isn't the best on gas, old as she is, but she'll still get ya there."

"Thanks, Dad. It'll be a really big help." Guilt trip. My conscious was producing the little angel and devil voices in my mind. I tried to shove the thoughts far away. *I need this opportunity,* I told myself. *I need a chance to find my own meaning.*

"You're welcome," he said, and gave me the expected handshake.

I got in the car, started the engine, and rolled the window down by hand. Yes, the car was that old. "I love you, guys," I said. "Thanks so much for everything." Everything that I knew I might have been throwing away.

"You deserve it and so much more," Mom said.

"I wish that were true," I whispered to myself.

We said bye again and I drove away. Whether they were waving or crying or hugging, I did not know. I didn't look in my rearview mirror.

CHAPTER SEVEN

Miraculously, even Luke and Bryce agreed that it would be stupid to take a road trip in which all of us drive separate vehicles. We would miss the fun of being cramped in one car with the luggage of three guys and no room to store it properly. I figured that the unpleasantness just had to be part of the experience. At least none of us were, like, super obese or anything. Bryce was a little chubby, but he drank a lot, so that was why. I called Luke who was already on the phone with Bryce, so it turned into this three-way conversation which was actually much less complicated than one would think.

Me: So, where am I supposed to meet you?

Bryce: My aunt's house. She's on too many drugs to notice two random cars parked behind her house. Hell, she's on too many drugs to even get out of bed except for when she needs to shoot up again or whatever she does. I don't know. I don't mess around with that shit. Nobody really visits her unless they're a customer. It's the perfect spot.

Me: How do I get there?

Bryce: Uh…

Luke: Goddamn, Bryce. Really!? She lives in the Hollow. You do not need to give directions to someone who lives in the Hollow to another person who also lives in the flipping Hollow. Jesus fucking Christ. Wade, you know that house on Missoula Avenue that always smells like fire and chemicals?

Me: Oh, yeah.

Luke: That's a meth lab and his aunt's house.

Me: Oh.

Bryce: Don't judge her, man.

I was afraid that her house would blow up while we were gone and take the shitty station wagon along with it. I knew that my parents would have killed me, and that's not a very epic way to die.

Mountain Hollow has a population of only 476 people. (It often changes because a stupid guy will get a stupid girl pregnant, they'd get married in the courthouse, he'd move in with her just to use her for food or whatever, then he'd beat her or find some other way to be a dick, and she'd kick him out.) Everyone *could* know everyone else if they wanted to, but we weren't one of those typical small towns that act like we are just a large group of BFFs. Most people just wanted to be left alone and most people respected that. There were quite a few people who made drugs or bought drugs from the people who made drugs and nobody did a thing about it. Not even the cops did much.

I put myself into the lone category of solitary genius. Population: Me. I lacked difficult and stimulating conversation with anybody there, so that got annoying. But it is what it is, I guess. Harvard was going to be filled with people who were probably even smarter than I am! I wanted to cry and drive toward Massachusetts and never step a foot in West Virginia ever again. I hated the Hollow. I hated it more than anything. For what it was and what it could never be. Luke and Bryce loved it there for some reason I'll never fully comprehend. After our trip, I knew they would settle back in Mountain Hollow like dust. You can stir them up all you want, and sure, they'll fly away for a while, but they will always fall back down. I didn't know why they were going to bother with any of it in the first place. It's as if Mountain Hollow is a magnet, and I'm the only one who can resist its gravity.

After about five minutes, I made it to Bryce's aunt's house. All the grass was dead and the dry, cracked dirt was visible beneath it, so I just drove through the yard. I didn't think she would mind. Luke was outside smoking. I was kinda paranoid, as dry as the ground was, that if he flicked a single ash everything below our feet would consume us with a hell-like flame. I turned off the ignition and went to meet him.

"Hey," I said.

"Hey, man" Luke said, and blew smoke in my face.

I nearly hacked out a lung. "Why do you feel the need to do shit like that? Goddammit."

"Because you need to toughen up." He took a long drag of his cigarette and blew the smoke away from me. "Better?"

"Whatever. Where's Bryce?"

"I think he's loading up the last crate of shine. He probably has a couple hundred jars of it in his trunk." He pointed to the van. "You know he wouldn't last a day without a sip of that stuff."

I should have expected it, but there I was, totally appalled. I tried my best not to look bothered and scared and pathetic. I really did. "I have a couple bags. Where are we putting our things, since his trunk is like an illegal rolling brewery these days."

"Just throw 'em in the back row of seats."

"Okay."

Bryce came out the back door, carrying a crate that must have weighed half of what he did, considering his face was red and all his major veins were protruding through his skin. "This is the last of it," he groaned through clenched teeth, and packed it in the trunk. It was dangerously full of alcohol and I did not like it.

"Yummy," I said sarcastically. "Anyway, you're sure my car will be safe here? The last thing we—and by we, I mean I—need is for my car to get hijacked and be all over the news. My mom is kinda too nice, so she would probably just assume I got lost, not that I was trying to ruin my life."

"It's fine. Seriously," Luke said, and threw a bag into Bryce's van. "I think that's all our stuff."

"Then why the fuck are we still standing here? Go go go go go!" Bryce said.
 I really wished I could share their excitement.

"Shotgun!" Luke shouted. I was more than okay with that. I wasn't about to wrestle him and claim my territory in the front, which is sorta childish if you ask me. I'm inherently distrustful of other drivers. Unless I am the one driving, because then it's necessary, I refuse to ride in the front. What if, what *if* somebody out there is thinking, *"God, life sucks. I don't know why I let it go on this long. I feel like offing myself by crashing into that hideous van?"* It could happen. Granted, if either vehicles are going fast enough, the back seat alone won't save my life. But still. At least if I have control of the wheel I can hope to make a quick decision that preserves my existence. Bryce was driving and that shine totally took away any reaction time he may have had to begin with. I was so scared I almost peed my smarty pants. I forgot to go before we left.

Something that also terrified me, no matter who was driving, was that the crappiest van to ever exist was supposed to make it to California. There was no way in hell it would work. My shitty station wagon was at least a little better than that van. There was a loud screech as Bryce pulled out of the driveway with more speed than necessary. Well, it wasn't really that fast, but the van couldn't handle much over fifty-five. It was going to be a long drive.

"Hey, Wade?" Bryce shouted two minutes into the drive. The windows were rolled down since the van lacked the ultimate blessing to mankind—air conditioning. The wind was loud.

"Yeah?"

"Can you reach behind you and find a Hello Kitty backpack?"

"What the fuck? You can't be serious." I wasn't judging or anything. I just didn't take him as the type of guy to be into that stuff.

"Nah, I'm totally messing with you. It's actually purple."

"Much better," I said. And his bags just *had* to be at the bottom. I lifted my bags beside me, since I currently had an entire row of seats to myself. I dug through loose oatmeal cream pies and bottles of Coke and jars of shine. It took me a few minutes, but I found it eventually. I handed it over the seat to Luke.

"What's in here?" Luke asked.

"Just a few CDs," Bryce said. "Find a Radiohead one. Don't matter which." *DOESN'T*! I wanted to say. I contained myself.

There were more than a few CDs in there. As Luke pulled out the albums that were not Radiohead, he threw them behind him. One hit my eye.

"What the hell is your problem?"

"Sorry, dude. Just don't be such a bitch," he said, and proceeded to aimlessly throw old CDs—Nirvana, REO Speedwagon, Journey—until he shouted "Eureka!"

"Put it in and turn it up," Bryce said.

Luke took the disk from its case and five seconds later I honest-to-God thought we were rear-ended and that the moonshine blew up like a thousand grenades and that I was already dead before we even made it out of Mountain Hollow. Born in Mountain Hollow. Died in Mountain Hollow. Accomplished nothing in between. I thought we were all dead. I heard screaming then laughs then cheers then more screaming. But then I noticed something. It was singing. A desperate attempt at singing.

"Wade, don't you know this song?" Luke screamed over the wind and loud rock music.

"Uh, I've never actually heard it. I kinda thought we died and that you guys were screaming or we were surrounded by the screams of sinners in hell. I was about to regret not being religious. I wasn't sure" I shouted back at him. It made my throat hurt.

"You are so freaking morbid! Bryce, turn it up louder!" So he did. They sang along with the album like they've done it a hundred times:

But I'm a creep.

I'm a weirdo.

What the hell am I doing here?

I don't belong here...

I don't know why, but in that moment, I felt like I totally connected to that song. I'm not saying that like some emo-poet person would say, "The words are, like, a part of your soul. Don't you feel that? Just breathe in the aura of sadness around you." That's not what I'm saying at all. But, what are any of us doing here? What did the artist mean by *here*? Maybe where he was in life or a certain place. Maybe the earth. Maybe he wanted to die. Maybe he was trying to matter to the world, but the world rejected him. Maybe he was trying too hard to matter. Maybe I was trying too hard to matter. Maybe mattering just needed to happen on its own. When people ask you, "What's the matter?" they're asking if something is wrong. Maybe trying to matter was wrong, too.

When the song was over, I asked them to play it again.

"See, Wade, you're finally feeling the awesome, aren't you?" Bryce asked.

"Yeah, I think I am." And I was actually smiling for the first time since the van left.

He played the song again and I badly sang along that time to the sad song that possibly answered all of my questions.

Every bit of guilt I had about the trip was gone.

CHAPTER EIGHT

Thirty minutes into the drive, Luke attempted to hook up the GPS. "Bryce, what bag is it in?"

"Uh, the black suit case. It has my name tag on it."

I knew my job. I found the suitcase and opened it. There was a GPS box that weighed less than air. I gave it to Luke and he opened it. "BRYCE, WHAT THE FUCK DID YOU DO!?"

That concerned me a little. Okay, a lot. "What?" he and I asked at the same time.

"There is no fucking GPS in this fucking box!"

Bryce hit his head repeatedly on the steering wheel. "I took it out of the box to look at it. Guess I forgot to put it back."

"You guess? What the hell, man?"

"I know. Sorry."

"Maybe if you wouldn't drink so much goddamn shine all the time shit like this wouldn't happen."

"I said sorry." He seemed kinda sad and I felt bad for him. "Now what are we gonna do?"

"I don't know. Why don't you ask our genius back there?" I know that you weren't supposed to be offended when someone called you a genius, but the way he said it was very offensive.

"Do either of you have a map?" I asked.

"God, no," Luke said. This isn't the frickin' 1800s. We have access to technology and assume we'll have it. I guess we should take fuckups into consideration."

"Luke, he's not a fuckup. He just fucked up. Yeah, it was kind of a major a fuck up, but it could have happened to any of us. Let it go. If we had a map, I could—" Then I thanked my lucky stars for my book addiction. I grabbed my duffel bag and took out the books until I found the history book I packed.

"What brilliant epiphany has struck you now?" Luke asked.

"I brought a few books. I think my history book has a map in it." I flipped through the appendix and held up a map of the United States. "Got it."

Luke literally climbed over his seat to hug me. "You're such a nerd, but I love you man! I love your weird habits."

"Um, thanks?" He was still squeezing. "Do you, uh, mind?"

"Oh, yeah. Sorry. I just got really pissed then suddenly really happy again."

"It's okay."

"I need to smoke. Bryce, can I smoke in here?"

"Yeah, just roll up the windows or I doubt it'll stay lit considering how fucking windy it is. Light one up for me, too."

"Sure. I brought, like, thirty packs. It'll last a couple months. Want one, Wade?"

"No, thanks."

"Whatever. They're here if you want one later." Luke lit one and put it between Bryce's lips. He lit another and breathed in deeply as he put the pack back in the glove box. I was truly amazed by how easily they both filled their lungs with gaseous chemicals without the slightest cough or wheeze. The smoke that drifted toward me was enough to make me have an asthma attack even though I don't actually have asthma. So, I asked.

"How do you do that?"

"Smoke?" Bryce asked. "Ain't nothin' to it."

"Yeah. Like, doesn't it make you feel all messed up?"

Luke laughed. "If you would have asked that five years ago, I would have said that smoking makes me feel like shit. Now, I don't even notice. I breathe it in, and I guess my body kinda needs it now. It's like pure oxygen to me. Keeps us alive."

"Aren't you worried about, like, getting cancer or dying or something?"

"Eh, no. Not really. We're all gonna die eventually. If you can't avoid something, you just have to face it." He took another drag of the cigarette, held the smoke in his mouth, and blew it out of his nose. That was kind of depressing for him to say. I remembered when he told me that he only acted like nothing bothered him. Maybe everything bothered him. It was sad to think about.

None of us spoke again for a while.

"Where are we?" Bryce asked. "I'm not really paying attention to signs or anything."

"Good thing I'm paying attention," I said. "There should be an exit in a few miles."

"Good. I gotta piss. And I'm kinda starving. Will you open an oatmeal cream pie for me and put it in my mouth?"

"Sure." I grabbed one from behind me and put the calorie-laden dessert in his mouth, as requested. I ate one, too. I wondered what kind of shit I would end up eating by the time the trip was over. I ate hotdogs, for

God's sake, but not pepperoni? I knew there was a problem with that. "Want one, Luke?"

"No, thanks. I'll wait. Where do y'all wanna eat?"

"Denny's," I joked.

"If you mention that again, I will grab your throat and hit you in the face with the GPS box. Might as well get some use out of it," Luke said.

"Are you guys okay with just stopping at a gas station and buying some crap?" Bryce asked.

"Uh, yeah," I said. I didn't really care as long as I could pee and eat something.

"Luke?" he asked.

"Sure. I don't mind."

Bryce actually remembered to use his turning signal when he turned on the exit ramp. We passed a sign that said MADISON GROVE: THE PRIDE OF WEST VIRGINIA. I have no idea why it said that. It wasn't really an exceptionally impressive town or anything. It was better than the Hollow, though. Anything was better than home. This town had a mall at least. And McDonald's. I hadn't been there since I was a freshman on our school's basketball team, the Mountain Hollow Howlers. Our mascot was a wolf. I sucked at basketball a lot. I kind of only joined so I could leave town for the weekend during State Finals. I was sadly content with being benched the entire time. Coach Karl (His name was appropriate. I hated him.) let me play once but yelled at me in the locker room because I missed a free throw when some other big guy fouled me. He called me a faggot then tripped me. The ref noticed, so he was benched the rest of the game. I quit the team, and the next year, Coach Karl wasn't there. Nobody even talked about him, so I assumed he got fired. I feared for the longest time that he was going to come to my house and kill me while I slept.

Bryce pulled into the parking lot of a Seven Eleven beside a gas pump. "I'll just get a few gallons for now. I don't know how long we've been driving."

"It's almost two," I said.

"Okay. Ya'll can go on in. I'll be there in a minute."

Luke and I walked in and a guy about our age at the counter said, quite unenthusiastically, "Hello. Welcome to Seven Eleven."

"Thanks," we said.
They were playing Taylor Swift, when she was still kinda country, from the intercom and I wanted to stab out my ears with the screwdrivers they had on display. Nobody cared that she was crying all over her guitar. Maybe Drew *just doesn't want you, Taylor.* "Don't you just hate her music?" I asked Luke.

"Am I straight? Very, very stupid question. I'm gonna go to the bathroom before Bryce makes it smell like horse shit."

"Good idea. I'm next." They had one of those bathrooms with only one stall. When Luke went to see if the door was unlocked, an extremely large man walked out. He was still in the process of zipping and buttoning his pants, so we knew he didn't wash his hands. "Oh. My. God."

"Bryce would have been better."

"Much better."

"Better than what?" Bryce asked, suddenly behind us.

I turned and pointed to the obese guy who was fingering absolutely everything he saw.

"Did he shit?"

"Why don't you check?" Luke suggested.

Bryce cracked the door and sniffed. "Yeah, he did. And there's piss on the seat."

"Now what the hell are we gonna do? I'm not going in there," I said.

"We can very sneakily use the women's bathroom," Bryce said.

"We can all keep watch for each other," Luke said. He looked like he was thinking. "If any of y'all see a girl when one of us is in there, shout 'Are you okay, honey?' toward the door."

"Why?" I asked.

"So we can tell her that our wife is very pregnant and throwing up all the time and has to pee every thirty seconds. Fellow women will feel compassion and back off."

"Not a bad idea," Bryce said.

"I know. I bet Wade would have never come up with such an awesome plan."

"I think you're right." I hated admitting that, but it was a genius idea that benefitted all of us.

Luke went first, then Bryce (who did shit but didn't really stink as much as the guy who was big and proud and didn't believe in cleanliness), then me. I checked my phone on the toilet since we were finally in a town with decent reception. I had, like, nine texts from Mom that were just different variations of:

I miss you, honey :'(Hope you're doing' OK out there by yourself. CALL ME!!!

She sounded like an obsessed girlfriend, to be honest. I called her. She picked up before it even had the chance to ring once.

Mom: Hi, baby!

Me: Hey, Mama.

Mom: How are you?

Me: Good. I just stopped at a Seven Eleven to stretch my legs and grab a snack.

Mom: That's good, honey. I miss you so much already.

Me: I miss you, too. How's Dad doing?

Mom: He misses you, even though he never says anything about it. Men, ya know?

I laughed.

Me: Yeah. I would know.

Then there was the code. I heard Luke shout, "Are you okay, honey?"

Me: I gotta go, Mama. I don't wanna lose too much time. I love you. Tell Dad hi.

Mom: I will. I love you more. Drive safe.

Me: 'Kay. Talk to you when I can.

I hung up and made a sound that hopefully resembled a pregnant lady throwing up vehemently. "I think so," I said in my best girl voice, which wasn't very good. I flushed the toilet and pretended to puke some more. I could hear the conversation going on outside the door. I had to try so hard to hold my laughter in. I made coughing and gagging sounds that only made me want to laugh even more.

Random Lady: Oh my goodness, is she okay?

Luke: She'll be all right. We're having our first baby. She's due any day now.

Random Lady: I remember when I had my first. Not too fun.

Luke: Yeah, it's been pretty rough on her. I know she's ready to have the baby.

Random Lady: Oh, well God bless her heart.

She seemed Christian. Southern Baptist, probably.

Luke: She's been a fighter, let me tell you that much.

Random Lady: Do ya know what ya'll are having?

Luke: Uh, no. We decided to wait for the big day.

Random Lady: How sweet! That's what my hubby and I did. You seem so young.

Luke: I'm twenty-three. My lovely wife and I married right out of college.

Random Lady: When you know you found the one, it's hard to wait too long.

Luke: Couldn't agree more. How many kids do you have?

Random Lady: Seven. My oldest is twenty-three and my baby is just fourteen months.

Luke: Wow. Well, congratulations on your wonderful family.

Random Lady: Thank you.

I made another puking sound and groaned a little.

Random Lady: Well, there's a restroom in the dollar store across the street, so I think I'll head on over there. Here's a little something to help you out. Good luck!

Luke: Thank you, ma'am.

A few seconds passed. "Okay, she's gone," Luke said.

I washed my hands and walked out. "That was a unique experience."

"She gave us fifty bucks."

"Are you serious?" Definitely a Christian.

"Yeah. Maybe we should do that more often."

I didn't really respond to that. I didn't intend to be a pregnant fraud for the rest of my life. "Where'd Bryce go?"

"He's getting a bunch of candy and chips and soda so we can wash them off before we buy them."

"Oh, good idea."

"God, I love you, honey," he said and rubbed my stomach.

"That's weird, dude."

"You were brilliant."

"I know, right?"

"Guys, come help me carry some of this stuff!" Bryce shouted.

We found him with his arms full of an assortment of junk. I took the bottles of soda, Luke took the candy, and Bryce kept the chips. We went into the men's bathroom this time since it probably had plenty of time to air out. We probably looked like three hormonal gays who wanted to pig out and do weird things in that bathroom. We checked to see if anybody was looking before we went in and locked the door. Without much concern for the safety of our items, we just threw the chips and candy in the sink and rinsed them all off for about five minutes. We did the same with several bottles of soda. They only had those hand dryers that blow hot air out for the sake of the environment. We didn't want warm soda or melted candy, so we didn't bother to dry them off. Each of us placed our soaking piles on the counter. "Do I wanna know?" the guy asked.

"Some guy didn't wash his hands then fondled half of the store. We were simply taking precautions," I said.

"I don't blame you. He comes in here, like, twice a day. I keep a can of air freshener behind the counter for that reason. You guys handled it really good."

"Thanks, man. We didn't know how you'd respond to a counter of wet products."

"No problem," he said, then scanned our stuff. He was actually really quick. We had a lot of things up there and he had them all scanned and bagged in under four minutes. We each paid ten bucks toward the total. "Have an awesome day," he said.

"You, too," all three of us said in unison.

We got back in the van with Luke driving this time. Bryce called shotgun, and again I didn't mind. I ate a little bag of Fritos, drank a Mountain Dew, and fell asleep to random mix CD I burned before a few days before we left for the trip. I desperately needed to get Taylor Swift out of my fucking brain.

CHAPTER NINE

By the time I woke up, it was pitch black outside. The floor of the van was littered with empty Mountain Dew bottles and candy wrappers and crumpled chip bags. I finally experienced Bryce's loud snore that Luke had only told me about. He was not exaggerating. His snoring was worse than my mom's. I stretched and sat up. "Where are we?"

"Uh, Kentucky. We're almost to Louisville. I'll probably stop there and we can figure out what to do," Luke said.

"You know how to use a map?"

"I'm not stupid. I just don't have to be better than everyone else."

"I never said I'm better than anyone."

"I didn't say I was talking about you." But I knew he was. And that shut me up fast. I watched the water of the Ohio River as we drove across the bridge. Reflections of the light from hotel windows and neon signs danced on the dark, glassy surface. I had never seen a real city in person. Everything about it was beautiful. Crossing the river was like crossing my own personal Rubicon. It was a decision I couldn't take back.

Luke led us into the heart of the city. People drunkenly walked through the streets, laughing. I wondered if any of those people were like me. If they wanted to escape the only place they've ever known but couldn't, so they drank and drank until they didn't even know their name. In a way, that would be a form of escape. Maybe it was mentally liberating. Maybe that's why Bryce drank so much. He and Luke could have wanted escape just as much as I did. We all handled things differently.

We were stuck behind a long line of traffic. The honking woke up Bryce. He yawned and asked for the time.

I checked my phone. "It's a little after one in the morning."

"That was the worst sleep ever," Bryce said. "Can we stop anywhere? I doubt we really have money for a hotel room."

"I was thinking we could just find a parking garage and sleep in the van. Maybe take a walk around the city or something. It's not like we have anywhere to be," Luke said.

"Dude, are you insane? We *cannot* sleep in a parking garage. In every fucking horror movie involving a killer, someone always gets sliced in a parking garage," Bryce so passionately pointed out. "If I'm gonna die, it's gonna be in Cali. Maybe I'll get into a surfing accident or some shit like that."

"I think we'll be okay," Luke said. There were garages all over the place. We settled on one that didn't seem intended for rich people and didn't seem too ghetto. We didn't want to get shot up or get our tires slashed. Luke parked on the second level and we all got out and walked around a little.

"While we're here, we might as well do something," I said.

"I'd suggest sneaking in a bar, but none of us have fake IDs," Bryce said.

I took my phone from my pocket and went on Google, thankful for reception again.

"What are you looking up?" Luke asked.

"Just something for us to do." I searched Louisville recreation and thousands of results came up. I typed in our current location to narrow down our options. "Do you guys like bowling?"

"Uh, yeah," Luke said.

"Bryce?"

"Yeah, but aren't all the bowling alleys probably closed by now?"

"Well, there's this place called Lois Lane's Bowling and More. It says they're open all the time. It's kind of a corny name, like probably superhero themed or whatever. But I'm hoping the *more* turns out to be food and not some comic book hall of fame," I said.

"Where is it?" Luke asked.

"It's on Grayson Boulevard. Do you remember seeing that anywhere?"

"Actually, it does kinda sound familiar. Is there an exact address?"

"Um, no. It just gives the street. Maybe it's new." I knew that it sounded more creepy and suspicious than new, we were supposed to be on an adventure. I wasn't about to be a pussy and ruin their time.

"We'll find out," Bryce said.

*   *   *

After walking a few blocks and getting weird looks from people when we asked for directions, we finally found it. It was a rundown brick building with a large neon sign on the roof that said LOIS LANE'S BOWLING & MORE. There were three women smoking outside, and I'm just gonna be honest, they looked like prostitutes. "They gotta have fun, too," Bryce said when I pointed them out.

"Oh, I'm sure they get plenty of that," Luke said. "Well, are we gonna go in or what?" To me, *what* sounded better than going in there. But we did.

The first thing I noticed was that the entire building was darkly lit and filled with smoke and strobe lights. We were immediately approached by another woman who also looked like a prostitute. I was beginning to doubt the name of the business. She asked our sizes. I told her I was nine. My feet were kinda small. Luke said ten, and Bryce said thirteen, which got a laugh from out prostitute attendant. "Follow me," she said. As we walked, she lit a cigarette and offered us one on the house. We all politely refused, even Luke. She led us down a hall and stopped in front of several doors. She knocked on three doors, each knock was the number of our shoe sizes. "Have fun, boys. And remember, strikes cost extra."

At that point, I was scared and just wanted to cry and ask my mom to pick me up. I don't care if I had to explain. I was just very freaked out. The three of us looked at each other before passing through the doors. I was greeted by yet again another woman, but more fully clothed this time. She was wearing a suit, like the kind a lawyer would wear. In spite of being a guy still in the prime of his youth, I was relieved to not see any of her parts popping out at me. I'm not gay, either. I just wanted a fat, sweaty bowling alley attendant that smelled vaguely of nacho cheese. I didn't think that was too much to ask for.

"Hello, there," she said. Her tone was more seductive than what I approved of.

"Hi," I awkwardly responded.

"What brings you in today?"

"My friends and I were passing through the city and we just kinda wanted to go bowling."

She laughed. I almost cried. "The bowling alley's been shut down since seventy-four. It's a whole lot more fun than what this dump used to be."

"Then, uh, what am I doing?"

She slipped off her suit to reveal a leather skirt and tight shirt that was cut in weird places and displayed the Superman symbol. *So, this is where the themes come in,* I thought. "Y'all just came to have a little fun. Ain't nothin' wrong with that."

"Actually, I think there's a lot wrong with that, at least at this point in my life. Maybe later when I'm unhappily married and unsatisfied." I didn't really believe that last part. I swear. I was just trying to use my sarcastic teenage wit to make light of the situation.

She began to perform what I think was a lap dance. That was not what I signed up for in life. Her ass was in my face and then she shook it a little. She then sat on my lap and I have no idea how to describe what she was doing. I didn't like it. It was weird and gross and it made me feel really guilty for some reason. "How's that for ya?"

"Actually, not too good." I kinda scooted out from underneath her and stood up. "I really can't do this. I'm seventeen. This probably isn't even legal." She didn't say anything. I walked out of the door and found Luke already waiting in the hall. Bryce came out a few seconds later and said, "I would have preferred bowling. Honestly. I was just kinda scared." Coming from Bryce, that was quite unexpected.

"I agree. Let's go," I said. We probably owed them a lot of money, but I didn't really care.

The women who I then decided were most definitely prostitutes after that experience were still outside smoking when we left. "Have fun, boys?" one of them asked. "That didn't take you guys very long."

"Um, no. Not really," Luke said. "It was sort of the worst experience of my life." And his life sucked. We started running as fast as we could. We were tired from driving and this was last thing we wanted. My healthy lungs were burning so badly from the strain. I can't imagine how Luke and Bryce were holding up. Their lungs were probably screaming for rest and nicotine. Once we could finally see the parking garage we started walking and wheezing and laughing for no reason but for the thrill of running from prostitutes in a city we've never been at two in the morning. I had crossed the Rubicon, and the change was drastic.

Back in the garage, I checked my phone. Mom hadn't texted, which surprised me. She was probably just learning to let me be independent. I checked my Facebook for no reason at all. I found Facebook to be somewhat shallow and pretentious. I preferred Twitter. I posted a Tweet of 139 characters for the enjoyment of my twenty-three followers about the weird experience of that day. We stayed up for a while and drank soda (even Bryce) and ate a couple peanut butter crackers. Luke licked his portion and applied them to his face. I took a picture just because it was pretty fucking hilarious. We all set alarms on our phones for noon so we wouldn't be stuck here during the night again.

Bryce always fell asleep first, which was annoying to Luke and I. I apologized to Luke when he and I were the only ones awake. "Luke?"

"Yeah?"

"Um, I just wanted to say sorry if I was being a douche earlier."

"More like every single day since we met. But you can't help it. Just smart person tendencies, I guess. Maybe I was jealous."

"Jealous of me?" I didn't know why.

"Yeah. I mean, you're really smart. You don't have to work for anything. I have to struggle to get a goddamn C on a test." He laughed, but I knew it wasn't the good kind of laugh.

"I wouldn't be jealous of me. Honestly. You and Bryce are so much more awesome than me. All I've ever done was try to please my dad. All I wanted was to be smarter than everyone else and make a lot of money I don't need and live somewhere like New York City, even if I hate it. And considering the way cities are in Kentucky, I'm sure I would hate it. I know you wanted to leave the Hollow because the past haunts you there. You just wanna get out. I wanted to leave to try to be better. And maybe I thought I was better than y'all and I'm sorry. Being smart or famous isn't as important as just living. I think I just fear dying and that's why I want to leave greatness behind and that's why I stopped truly living." That took a lot of humility to say. More than you could ever imagine. But it felt sort of good.

"Not bad, Wade. Not bad at all. I knew you'd come around."

"I'll get there eventually."

CHAPTER TEN

We left the parking garage at 12:24 after a quick and odd breakfast of Oreos and Sprite. The traffic was worse than we hoped. We hadn't factored in the lunch rush. By one o'clock, all of our phones were dead. None of us remembered to pack car chargers. It was my turn to drive and I had enough soda and artificial sugars in my system to keep me awake for the next seventy-two hours, I imagined. The map in my book was fairly small, so, with utmost hesitation and hyperventilation, I tore out the page, chewed a couple sticks of gum, and stuck the map to the steering wheel at Luke's recommendation.

I kept the van at its safe speed of fifty-five and drove and drove and drove down the highway in a blurred line that never seemed to end...

EDMONTON, INDIANA

There was only corn. I drove through the entire state and saw nothing but barns and corn. I wasn't used to being surrounded by tall vegetables. It almost creeped me out and made me a little sleepy, but I fought the fatigue. "Dude," Bryce said.

"Me?" I asked, considering there were two other dudes in the van beside him.

"Yup. I think this is where popcorn comes from. Like, they grow the entire world's ultimate movie food in this miserable little town. Who would've thought?"

I'm sure that endless tunnel of corn of either side of us was just getting to his head. There's no way that one town could grow possibly one of the most popular snack foods ever. I've seen overweight people at movie theaters go back for popcorn (which was probably more butter than actual popcorn) more than ten times in a single showing. I mean, they probably miss most of the move. I have no idea why they just don't go to the store and buy a couple hundred boxes of microwave popcorn so they can conveniently make it at home rather than pay for a movie they hardly acknowledge. But whatever floats their boat. Those people probably ate an entire field of corn, so as ridiculous as Bryce's thought was, I entertained it. "Yeah, it's pretty incredible," I said.

"Corn makes the best whiskey, too. We should go pick some. I wonder if I can make shine out of it."

"Bryce, that's a terrible idea."

"Plus that's stealing," Luke said.

"Yeah," I agreed. "We wouldn't want to deprive the world of movie lovers from their favorite food, would we?"

"No," he said in a way that sounded exactly like a pouting child. "I want popcorn now."

"We don't have a microwave, smart one." Thank you, Luke, for pointing out the obvious.

"Duh. God, do you think I'm an idiot?"

"Uh, well…" Luke said.

"Don't answer that. They make the kind that's already popped."

"We're not stopping for a bag of popcorn," I said.

"UGH! Fine." Bryce was never good at arguing. "Do you think there are children in there?" he added a few minutes later. Neither Luke nor I responded.

SPRINGFIELD, ILLINOIS
I slept.

RIVERSIDE, MISSOURI
I slept.

PEYTON CITY, KANSAS
Bryce stopped the van at a rest area. The vending machine contained mini bags of pre-popped popcorn. Bryce had a fit of excitement and bought every bag they had and left a note apologizing for buying all the popcorn. His note was stuck to the vending machine with a wad of gum. We all finally changed clothes for the first time since we left. I peed. Luke peed. Bryce clogged the toilet. We ran like the dickens. No, only old people say that. I am full of youth and living in the moment. I don't even know what the dickens is. I'll just say that we ran for our lives.

PUEBLO, COLORADO

The mountains were even worse in Colorado than they were in West Virginia. We switched drivers early because we didn't really trust Bryce's driving here. Luke took over. He and Bryce smoked again for the fiftieth time. For the fiftieth time, I had a little asthma attack. They didn't seem to notice.

My mind was restless. The lack of mental stimulation was driving me insane. "Anybody wanna play travel Scrabble?" I asked. They both laughed and said they never scored anything higher than a sixty-five on a spelling test in their entire lives.

"I'll go easy on you."

So we played. We each kept eight letter tiles in our hands so we wouldn't lose them. Bryce drew a B, so he went first. He played the word cat.

I held the board up so Luke could see. All he did was add an S to Bryce's word. Trying to keep my promise of going easy on them, I played the words catsup. It hurt my brain even worse to use such words, but I promised. I have no clue how the two of them would have survived college. I'm sorry to say that they would have been better off as gypsies for the rest of their lives. I don't think they're allowed to go to college anyway. They're just like skimpily dressed, non-religious Amish people.

I won the game with words like catsup, giraffe, and bowl. Don't ask me how. The smartest person in the world couldn't answer that question accurately.

CASTLETON, UTAH

I drove again. The desert was almost worse than the corn back in Indiana. I felt like aliens were going to descend from the clouds, steal the van, eat our eyes, and study our brains. Then science kicked in and I realized how highly unlikely that was. But sometimes science was wrong. I've been wrong before, too. Luke and Bryce were asleep. It was just me and multiple millions of particles of reddish-brown dust.

The desert filled the van with suffocating heat, making it necessary to want the windows down. But at the same time, I could feel the sand flying into my eyes as I drove. I regretted not packing a pair of sunglasses.

I ultimately decided to keep the windows rolled down. I pulled over to the side of the road and took off my shirt to help stay cool.

I didn't really help much.

LAS VEGAS, NEVADA

Bryce was driving and we unanimously agreed to stop in Las Vegas. It was a little out of our way, but how could we not stop there? While we were doing unwise things, we figured that we might as well have done the ultimate unwise thing and take a trip to Vegas. "Can we find a McDonald's?" I asked.

"We're in Vegas. There are probably ten of them on every block," Luke said. "We should go somewhere fancy. I'm sure if we all paid fifty dollars or something, we could manage something at least a little better than McDonald's."

"True," I said. "But it's, like, four something in the morning. Nothing is gonna be open. We could find a hotel somewhere and crash in the lobby."

"All the hotels in Vegas are probably run by stuck-up bitches. There's no way they'll let us stay in the lobby," Bryce said.

"Well, if you just let me do the talking, we'll see what happens," I said.

"This better work. I can't spend another night in a parking garage. I couldn't sleep at all. Too much paranoia," Bryce said.

"You are such a liar. You were snoring for, like, nine straight hours," Luke said. I was thinking the same thing, but I wasn't going to say it.

*   *   *

We found a hotel called The Louis. Sounded fancy enough. We grabbed our bags from the trunk, each of us took turns changing into our nicest outfit, and we walked right in like we owned the place. Within seconds of entering the door a concierge offered to take our bags. We asked to speak to a manager first. He directed us to the front desk. As planned, Luke and Bryce didn't say a word and with my best English accent, I spoke. "Hello, my name is Edward Carson and these are my friends Phillipé and Carlos (Bryce was maybe tan enough to pass as a Carlos) from France and Spain. I'm from England and the only one who speaks English."

"Good evening, Mr. Carson," the manager guy said in a southern accent.

Even though we were in Nevada, I almost expected a man like him to have a European accent for some reason. "How may we be of service to you?"

"We have only currency from our home countries. We are foreign exchange students on the way to study and begin our lives at the University of California. I think we have plenty of money to exchange for American dollars when we reach California, but not until then. Would we be able to perhaps spend the night here and sleep in the chairs in your lobby?"

"Allow me to look something up in our database," he said.

"Yes, of course." I looked over at Bryce, who seemed as if he were going to explode with laughter at any second.

He typed and scrolled for a few minutes. My heart was pounding the whole time and I had no idea why. Probably because I was actually lying well for once in my life. I didn't even feel that guilty. I didn't know if that was a bad thing or just something normal for someone my age. "We have one room open on the ground floor. It will be small because it is one of our less expensive rooms. I would be happy to allow you to use it tonight. It should be sufficient for what you and your friends need."

"Are you sure? I wouldn't want to impose, really," I said.

"I am absolutely sure. You seem like a very nice group of boys."

"Thank you so much, sir. I appreciate it very much. If my friends could understand a word of what we were saying, they would be very happy. I'll explain it to them shortly. I speak both Spanish and French. A little Lithuanian and German, too. I just haven't had the need to use them yet." I smiled at him. He was right where I needed him.

"Very well." He snapped his fingers and the concierge came back to take our bags to our room. The manager gave me a key to our room and I slipped it into my pocket.

"We'll be back later tonight. We don't have to leave too early in the morning."

"Enjoy your time in Las Vegas," he said.

"Oh, I am very sure we will, sir. Thank you again and have a good night."

"Holy fuck, I can't believe that just happened," Luke said. We were back in the van and driving through the city.

"Me either," I said.

"How in the hell did you do that?" Bryce asked.

"I honestly don't know. I didn't think it would work. I figured one of you would burst out laughing before I finished my little speech."

"It was brilliant," Luke said. "Well, I think we'll have the fancy meal covered for tomorrow morning. Might as well hit up the McDonald's drive-through."

"Good. That little spiel made me hungry," I said.

Luke was damn near right when he said there would be ten of them on every block. We just chose one randomly since every McDonald's on the face of the earth was exactly the same—greasy, poorly managed, and cheap. "Hello, thanks for choosing McDonald's," a lady said from a speaker. "How may I help you?" She sounded kinda happy for working at a fast-food restaurant this late. I would've been like, "What the *fuck* do you fatties need from McDonald's at four in the morning? You just gotta make my already sucky life a little suckier, don't you?" Kudos to her.

"Umm, we'll need a couple minutes," Luke said.

"Take your time, sugar."

"What do y'all want?" Luke asked us.

"Uh, just a dollar cheeseburger without the cheese and add extra ketchup. I'll have a large order of fries, too," I said.

"I'm not even going to ask about what you just said. Bryce, what do you want?"

"Order me a twenty piece nuggets and two large fries. Oh, and a large Coke and a couple of them apple pies. You ever tried those pies? It's like heaven inside you."

"Every human being in America has tried those pies. And I wouldn't really compare them to heaven. Maybe purgatory with the hope of making it to heaven one day, but not quite heaven itself," Luke said.

"Then you have never eaten one. Or your taste buds are dying. Either way, you're mental, bro."

Luke just rolled his eyes. Sometimes that's all you could do when talking to Bryce. "Okay, we're ready," he said.

"All right. What can I get for you?"

"We'll take a twenty piece nuggets, two large fries, a large Coke, and two apple pies."

"You'll save seventy-nine cents if you make that a combo meal with an extra fry," the lady said.

"Sure. Let's do that. And I'll have a dollar cheeseburger without the cheese for my special friend, here. Add extra ketchup to that one, please. We'll also have two more large fries, two dollar chicken sandwiches without the mayo, and a couple things of ranch."

"Okay, we have a…" And then she repeated the order back to us. You don't really need to hear that again. "Will that be all for ya tonight?"

"Uh, yeah. I think so."

"Okay. Your total is thirteen dollars and seventy-seven scents. Pull up to the next window and we'll have that ready for you in just a few minutes."

"Thank you," Luke said.

We must have been the only ones there because they gave us our food pretty darn fast. I ate my fries three at a time and savored my cheeseburger without the cheese. I was impressed that the lady didn't ask for more explanation regarding the request. If only every restaurant employee in the world were like her. It was drenched in enough ketchup to appease all the toddlers in the world that have ever lived with their weird apple habits. (Every time I see a little kid with apples in a restaurant, they dip their apples in ketchup. It looks disgusting, but whatever gets them to eat the fruit.)

Considering the lateness of the hour, we just ate in the parking lot. "I never thought I would ever be eating sucky food in Vegas with my two awesome friends," I said.

"Me either," Luke said with several fries loaded with ranch sticking out of his mouth.

"I didn't even think the van would make out of the state," Bryce said. "This piece of shit did good."

"Do you wanna get back to the hotel? We should sleep in an illegally-obtained real bed while we have the chance," I said. "Then it's back to parking garages."

We all shuddered at the thought.

CHAPTER ELEVEN

When we went back to our room in The Louis, I was totally taken aback with what I saw. "What the hell are you guys doing?"

"Jumping...on the ...bed," Bryce said with deep breaths between his words.

"Well, stop it!"

Luke continued to jump as he spoke. "Have you seriously never jumped on a bed before?"

"No, of course I haven't. It's a dangerous activity that injures at least fifteen kids a year! Don't you watch those medical shows? Like, these kids jump on their beds and then they fall off and land really badly on their arm and it just snaps in half. We can't afford to go to a hospital if you do something stupid."

"Nope, never seen those shows a day in my life," Bryce said. "I don't have cable. I'm pretty content with watching Forrest Gump on my VCR for the rest of my days. I like that movie."

"Well, if y'all get hurt, you still have to drive," I said.

Luke jumped off the bed. It was a good thing we were on the ground floor or we probably would have been kicked out. "Come on. It's, like, the fluffiest bed in the entire universe. Literally all the goodness in the world is contained in this mattress."

I rolled my eyes. "I'm just gonna go take a shower. I feel like a homeless person." I was actually growing stubble. I can't remember the last time I looked in the mirror and saw a single hair on my face, let alone several at once. It wasn't bad, really. I shaved it anyway. I knew that there was no way I could have helped us acquire another hotel room, so I wouldn't have been able to shave and feel clean again for a while. I didn't want to look like a Viking or a creeper. After my shower, I thought I was going to die right there. I didn't even have the chance to skateboard down a totally scary mountain. They were eating Skittles *and* jumping on the bed.

"You guys are really trying to kill me, aren't you?"

"Nope. We kinda need you here, nerd. You got us this badass room," Bryce said.

"Come jump with us. If you can't jump on a bed, there's very little in life you'll be able to do. I'm not asking you to jump out of a motherfucking airplane into the Grand Canyon filled with sharks."

Bryce was right. I would never in a million years be able to accomplish awesome metaphorical mountain feats. "Yeah, okay." I took a deep breath and sat on the bed. I stood slowly to keep my balance and it wasn't really as terrifying as I thought it would be. "You weren't exaggerating about the fluffiness," I said and jumped. I WAS JUMPING ON A BED! LIKE WHAT THE HELL WAS THIS LIFE!?

"I told you," Luke said. He held out his bag of Skittles. "Want some?"

"Uh, I don't really know if I'm ready for that yet…"

"Not ready to eat candy? Seriously? It's not a big deal." To me it was.

"I've never had one in my entire life. For seventeen years and several months I have managed to keep my body devoid of edible lies."

"Just one?" Bryce said, now holding out his bag. This was extreme peer-pressure. Normal teens pressure with and give in to drugs and alcohol and sex with random people at parties you're not even supposed to be at. Nobody in the entire history of ever has been pressured to eat Skittles, let alone *a* Skittle. For the first time, I kind of realized how stupid I was being. Starving African children would kill to be able to hold a Skittle without even being allowed to eat it. There I was in Sin City, in a hotel room that we managed to get because of my sin of lying, and I was refusing to eat a candy that was glorified by the same sin I committed: lies.

"You know what? What the fuck ever," I said. I grabbed Bryce's bag and poured every last Skittle in my mouth. I almost choked, but I didn't. I stopped jumping for a second and just stood there on the bed. "Oh. My. God."

"I know, right?" Luke said.

"Why did nobody tell me that these are kinda better than cheese burgers without cheese and extra ketchup!? Why did you allow me to be so unfortunate for so long?"

"Because you always act like a stuck-up prude when we mention anything fun?" Bryce said.

"Yeah, I think that sounds about right," Luke agreed.

"Sorry," I said, with my mouth full. I was genuinely amazed by how good lies can actually taste. I collapsed on the bed and either in a fit of happiness or a fit of rage, I shoved my face in a pillow and just burst into laughter.

"Umm?" Luke was just as confused as I was about the situation.

"I don't even know right now, man. I really don't," I said. At some point between my little tantrum and being called a real man by Luke and Bryce, I fell asleep on the ridiculously comfortable bed that I lied (without feeling any remorse whatsoever—huzzah!) to obtain. My stomach was full of the lies of assorted artificial, non-rainbow flavors that I would probably eat forever and ever until I got sick of them. And at that point, it seemed highly improbable.

*   *   *

"Shit shit shit shit! Guys, wake up!" I said when I finally rolled over and accidentally fell off of the bed. It was a tight fit for all of us to sleep on one bed, but we made the best of it. It was like the gay-but-straight sleepover every guy secretly wanted to experiment with but rarely had the chance to do.

"God, what?" Luke asked. He sounded pissed and tired, which was probably a good description of all three of us at that point.

"It's, like, almost two. We gotta go."

"No no no!" Bryce whined.

"What?" Luke asked him.

"We missed free and fancy breakfast, man. That's the only reason I put up with some rich hotel. Rich people piss me off for some reason. I don't know why. They just do. Like they have a monopoly on all the world's awesome. What kinda shit is that?"

"Wealthy shit," I said. "But right now we have a monopoly on getting the hell out of here before they realize we're not European kids on the way to college."

We packed our bags as fast as we could, not bothering to be neat about it. Bryce grabbed his bag of leftover McDonald's from the mini-fridge and put it in his backpack of CDs. I ran into the bathroom and almost slid to my demise on the wet floor. (Luke and Bryce actually took a shower, believe it or not.) I tossed my shaving kit haphazardly into my suitcase and counted to make sure I had the same number of clothing articles as when we arrived. I got dressed in a wrinkly outfit that my dad would have glared at me for wearing. The shirt looked absolutely terrible and I would have normally cared, but we were kind of in the biggest hurry in all the hurries of the world.

"Where the fuck are my cigarettes?" Luke shouted. He was looking in the fridge. I had no idea why they would be in there.

"I don't know," I said.

"Of course you don't know. You just so casually know all the bullshit that isn't gonna help us in this situation, but you don't know this one thing."

"Calm the fuck down. You have, like, a ton in the van."

"I don't care what I have, dammit. A poor man just can't leave behind perfectly good cigarettes in a hotel," he said.

"I found them!" Bryce shouted. "They were in my leftovers. Don't ask why because I have no fucking clue. But yeah. Here you go," he said and tossed them to Luke.

He was really about to light one up right then and there but I had to tell him that was the stupidest thing ever and could quite possibly set off the smoke detector in the room. He mumbled something that I couldn't hear and at this point we all had better things to worry about than Luke's attitude problem.

When we quadruple checked everything three times, we left the room in decent shape. We all had charged cell phones, which was excellent. I pretended to speak French as we were walking into the lobby. "Remember," I whispered to Luke and Bryce. "Don't say anything because you are extremely foreign and couldn't speak a syllable of English to save your lives."

"Ah, good afternoon, Mr. Carson. How was your stay?" the same manager asked.

"It was wonderful," I said, in my poor English accent and handed him the key.

"Thank you," he said.

"No, my friends and I should be the ones to do all the thanking. Your offer was very generous."

"It was our pleasure, sir. Would you like help carrying your bags to your vehicle?"

"Uh, no. But thank you anyway. You have done so much more than enough."

"Well, have a safe trip and welcome to America."

"Thank you. You indeed have made us all feel very welcome," I said.

We walked out of the hotel with confidence, as we imagined Europeans with pretentious accents would do. It was my turn to drive so I tossed my bags in the back seat and started the van. Luke called shotgun, to which Bryce replied with, "Fuck you, man. Gotta beat the chubby one, don't you?" I don't know why riding shotgun was such a big deal. I made a mental note to search the origin online later. For the first time since we left Mountain Hollow, Bryce took a few sips of his shine. He only drank half a jar, which I guess wasn't too bad. He offered Luke and I a jar. Luke just finished off the other half of Bryce's. I refused because it was stupid and illegal to drink and drive. If, in another universe, it happened to be smart and legal, I still wouldn't have done it. Kinda because of the whole reminding me of bleach and nail polish remover thing.

I drove down this road that was basically like a strip-mall of casinos and bars and fancy live shows starring the world's best opera singers and dog shows and acrobats and whatever. None of those things sounded the least bit appealing because I liked my ears, watching various tiny dogs run through tunnels for no reason but sucky entertainment is a waste of money, and seeing people twist themselves the way the human body is not intended kinda grosses me out, even when I occasionally watch it on TV during times of severe boredom.

I pulled the van over so that we could eat some of the junk food we still had left. I ate a bag of Cheetos and ten Skittles. I didn't wanna go overboard with my newly found love. Bryce ate, like, four packs of crackers, the rest of his food from the night before, and a few Oreos. Luke said he was okay with just a cigarette, one Oreo, and a sip of Coke. That was probably why he was so skinny, like skinnier than me. It couldn't have been healthy. I'm sure he didn't care.

I turned the keys but the van wouldn't start back up. "That is really bad," I said.

"What?" Bryce asked. It was his van, after all.

"Uh, it won't start."

"How are we doing on gas?" Luke asked.

"We have more than half a tank left." I turned the key. There wasn't even a clicking sound to give us hope. "Maybe she just couldn't make it any farther."

"What are we supposed to do?" Luke asked. "We're in the middle of Vegas. We've still got a while to go until we reach California."

"Maybe we can try to walk and find a mechanic," Bryce suggested. "The battery just might need a jump."

"Yeah," I said. "And maybe this is where we begin our lives."

CHAPTER TWELVE

As we wandered around Las Vegas, I actually learned something new, not that it'd help me later on in life. I found out that you shouldn't even *think* about going to Vegas unless you're ridiculously rich or plan on becoming ridiculously rich by gambling away your lack of wealth. We went to, like, at least eight garages with absolutely nothing to show for it. I was kinda pissed off. All of us were. As to be expected, the mechanic asked us for the make and model of the vehicle we were driving. When Bryce said that it was a 1984 van, they refused to even look at it. One guy even had the nerve to tell us that they only work on Ferraris and Audis and other rich shit like that. He laughed at us and told us to leave. After a while, we just gave up. The three of us walked back to the van that surprisingly hadn't been ticketed, and sat in it. There was really nothing else we could do. "Does anybody know what time it is?" Bryce asked. "I'm too lazy to check right now."

I clicked my phone. "It's almost seven."

"I'm kinda too scared to ever go bowling again," Luke said. "So, that's out. Like, for the rest of my life. I'm much too young to never go bowling again. I even have my own frickin' ball. But back in Kentucky, that ruined me for life, man."

I laughed a little. "I have a pair bowling shoes for some reason. I don't know why. My dad bought them for me for my birthday one year. Anyway, I don't blame you." We were bored out of our mind, so I made the appropriate nerd suggestion. "Do you guys wanna play another game of Scrabble?"

"Hell, no," Bryce said. "That sort of took away any sense of pride I might have had left."

"It's wasn't that bad," I said. I knew that wasn't true, but it would have been rude to agree.

"Are you kidding?" Luke said. "It fucking sucked. Your score was better than mine and Bryce's together. We would've lost if we cheated."

"Fair enough," I said.

"I'm hungry," Bryce said.

"Of course you are. I'm hungry, too, so you must be starving, "I said. "Y'all wanna take a walk and find something relatively cheap but not even similar in food-genre to McDonald's, Denny's, or Pizza Hut?"

"Yeah. Maybe Taco Bell," Luke said.

We grabbed our money and Bryce locked the van, lest our few possessions be stolen. "Let's go get us some Americanized Mexican food," he said. He was accurate in saying that. There is nothing even remotely Hispanic about Taco Bell.

It wasn't difficult to find one at all. I looked up Las Vegas Taco Bell on Google and there were, like, twenty results for Vegas and a few of its suburbs. There was one not too far away from where we were. Normally, we just would've used the drive-thru, but that obviously wasn't an option.

I used the GPS on my phone and we walked there. It took about thirty minutes. We could smell the food outside the restaurant and it made my stomach growl. It had been years since I last had Taco Bell.
Luke and I stood amazed as Bryce ordered and actually consumed twelve hard-shell tacos, two burritos, and an order of cinnamon twists. I ate one soft-shell taco, one hard-shell taco, and a small Mountain Dew, that really good kind that only Taco Bell has. Luke had two burritos and a churro. Bryce was finished eating before Luke and I were half-way through our meal, which scared me a little. When he ran out of money (which was bound to happen sooner or later), I was afraid his cannibalistic instincts could have kicked in. I liked life. There were much better ways to die. Well, less pitiful ways than being eaten alive by one of your best friends.

"Now what?" Luke asked.

Bryce burped. "That was some good shit." Then he stood up and walked to the bathrooms, licking his fingers the whole time.

"For once in my life, I honestly don't know," I said. The trip kinda brought out a lot of things in me that I didn't know. It made me somewhat uncomfortable. Like, knowing just about everything was what made me better, I guess. If I don't know everything there is, being a genius is no different than being like anyone else. I still had to learn and experience things, too.

"I say we just sleep in the van for, like, infinity and then figure out what to do many infinites later," Luke said.

"I feel like we'd be all be extremely dead even half an infinity from now, but I agree."

"Sounds good enough for me," he said.

Bryce came back from the bathroom and informed us that Taco Bell passes right through him. "I am not gonna for such a long time, as full as I am."

Luke and I knew that wasn't true.

Our legs were kinda hating on all of us then on our way back to the van. The burning was like, "What now bitches? How do you like it?!" If I weren't afraid of looking like a schizophrenic psycho, I would've yelled at my legs and told them to shut the fuck up and do their job. It probably took us an hour to walk less than a goddamn mile.

When we finally made it to the van, I nearly dropped on my knees and praised a Higher Being for that miracle. Bryce reached into his pocket then there was a long line of cursing. Like every single curse word ever muttered by every human ever.

"God, what the hell is your problem now?" Luke asked.

"I left the keys in the van," he sort of mumbled.

"What?" Luke asked.

"I said I left the keys in the motherfucking van!"

"I heard you, idiot. That was more of the surprised and pissed off type of what. Ya know, like what the hell did you do?"

"It was an accident, man."

"Maybe we can try to pick the lock," I said.

"You know what? Fuck it," Bryce said. A few feet from where we were parked, there was this decorative thing in front of a building filled with rocks and flowers. He picked up one of the biggest rocks and came back over.

"Uh, please don't tell me that's your best idea," I said.

Bryce didn't say anything. He raised the rock above his head and threw it as hard as he could at the windshield. "There," he said, and climbed in through the window, which was very unsafe considering the jagged pieces of glass that were left behind. Judging by another line of fucks and such, I'm pretty sure he got cut. Luke and I just stood there, not really desiring to slice open our arms for the sake of sleeping in a van that would no longer even protect us from the elements. "God, you guys are pussies," Bryce said and opened the sliding door so that we could more comfortably get it.

Bryce was in the driver's seat and Luke called shotgun for no reason at all. I took my happy place in the back seat. No one said anything for an awkwardly long time. I just stared at my phone for a while and then texted my mom that class was going really well, that my advanced math class was a little hard but manageable, and that I was sorry for not talking to her and Dad that much because I was so busy. That may have been the most lies I have ever told at one time. But it was for their benefit. If the text would have said that I'm just stranded in Vegas with the two people Dad hates more than anybody in the world, they probably would have had heart attacks and died on the spot. I'd rather not be responsible for their death and/or hospitalization. So, I lied only out of necessity.

After an hour or so, Bryce was the one to talk first. "I can't deal with this shit for the rest of my life. I can't. Do you guys wanna go drink? I have a ton of shine. Might as well get something good out of it." The good thing about throwing up drunkenly on strangers in Vegas is that most of the people there were probably already drunk themselves, so it's not like anyone would actually care about vomiting or being vomited upon.

"Yeah. Nothing sounds as good as that does right now," Luke said.

I didn't say anything since I don't, like, really drink large amounts of alcohol for the pure enjoyment of it. But I went anyway. There was no way I would have just stayed there by myself. A rabid homeless guy could have climbed in through the windshield and bit my arm, thus contaminating me with Rabid Hobo Disease. That probably wasn't a real thing, but imagine a doctor telling you that you have stage IV RHD. It'd sound damn real and damn life-threatening and I bet you'd do some messed up shit like jumping out of airplanes and stuff.

Bryce took out the CDs from his purple backpack and replaced them with five bottles of his moonshine. Luke brought a bag of many packs of cigarettes, and I brought my duffel with books and Scrabble just because they took a few things. It didn't seem like they were coming back.

I looked at the van one last time, and smiled. Everyone else was pissed off at the world. But not me. I didn't care about a single thing. Something told me that everything was going to be okay.

CHAPTER THIRTEEN

I have to admit that while we were walking down the highway
sometime around midnight, I was a little concerned with drunk drivers.
I knew they probably wouldn't see us. If they did see us, by some
miracle, their inhibitions would be much too impaired to think, "Hey,
look at that fine group of boys all full of youth and poverty. I think I'll
slow down to a legal speed and move over a little so I don't smear their
bodies all over the road with my bad driving." If that were the case, the
world would be a much better place.

We walked a while longer and just stopped on this overpass because,
well, I guess it seemed like a good place to rest and think. It overlooked
the entire city. The people were nothing but mobile specks from where
we stood. We leaned over the railing and I was genuinely terrified in
that moment. You'd think that living in West Virginia, a state that was
basically one giant mountain, heights would be the least of my fears.
Nope. I've never been hiking in the mountains or climbed anything at
all. I like the ground. I like flat surfaces and I like that I can trust gravity
to keep me from floating away into the vast expanse of outer space.
Anything else terrified me.

Bryce took a jar of shine from his bag and took a drink. He passed it to
Luke. "Want some?"

"Yeah. Thanks." He drank a little less than Bryce did, but not by much.

Then he handed it to me, which surprised me. Luke knew I didn't drink much, especially not moonshine. But I took it anyway. I just kinda looked at it for a minute, amazed by how it looked exactly like water. I wondered if I could just take a sip and convince myself it wasn't what it really was. I sniffed it and knew it was a stupid thought. Luke and Bryce were staring down at the city, not even acknowledging my breakthrough moment of a lifetime. I put the jar to my lips and sipped slowly. I held it in my mouth and swished it around, allowing my mouth to become familiar with the taste. It was the worst thing I ever had. A hundred times worse than cigarettes or fancy cigars.

I hesitantly swallowed and I could feel it burning my esophagus in a way that was entirely unfamiliar. It was weird. It kind of made me feel literally warm. I took another drink, going through the same slow process. I did it again and again until the jar was empty. It wasn't good or anything, yet I continued to drink it. I thought about the reason why people drank, even though it was bad. It wasn't fun or free or healthy at all. It took away *you.* It made you act differently. It made you forget things you've known your entire life, like your address or name. That thought gave me an idea. Maybe forgetting was the point of drinking. Maybe people who drink, no matter what they make themselves out to be, all have demons that they face when they are alert and aware of their reality. Like, drinking wasn't necessarily something they loved to do for fun. It was a necessary means of escaping the life they didn't want. It was a better escape than just dying, because life, no matter how much it sucked, could get better and was always better than not existing at all. But that was hard for me to think. My life wasn't bad at all. I had it so much better than they did.

Bryce's life sucked pretty badly. He drank all the time. Luke's life wasn't too great either. So sometimes he drank, too. I didn't know why I was drinking, though. I didn't think there was anything I was trying to escape from. Well, I was trying to escape Mountain Hollow, but I had done it already. I left and maybe I wouldn't even go back for a visit. The only thing there was left to escape from was…me.

I gave the empty jar to Bryce who looked just as shocked as I felt. "Did you drink that?" he asked.

"Uh, yeah. I did. It wasn't that bad, really."

"I'm proud of you, man. Maybe you ain't so bad after all."

"Maybe not," I said.

Luke laughed and lit a cigarette. "Don't end up like Bryce unless you plan on cleaning up your own puke."

"Can we not talk about that?" Bryce asked.

"Don't worry. It probably won't become a regular thing for me."

"Right," Bryce said. He took another jar from his backpack and held it out from the overpass. He looked to make sure no cars were coming and then he let it fall. We could just barely see the glass reflecting the colors of the neon lights when hit the ground, shattering into hundreds of irreparable fragments.

"What the hell was that for?" Luke asked. I was curious, myself.

"For the road," he said.

I found that to be overflowing with metaphorical resonance. I doubt they saw it that way, but it was kind of remarkable. Luke took an unopened pack of cigarettes from his bag and stared at it for a minute. He opened the pack and dropped it from the overpass. The cigarettes fell out of it and blew around on the ground where they fell. He looked sad as hell for doing it, but he did. "For the road," he said.

They both looked at me, expecting me to do the same thing. I didn't really have anything with me, though. But I remembered that my duffel had all my favorite books in it. Isn't that what Luke and Bryce threw? They threw their favorite things. God, I knew it was gonna suck. I unzipped my bag and took out my copy of *Slaughterhouse Five.* I flipped through the yellowing, torn pages one last time. I skimmed the notes that lined every margin of every page. I reread the highlighted lines and, like, almost cried. It was pathetic. I had another copy at home, of course. But I couldn't go home. There were thousands of used and new copies waiting to be purchased. I could easily get another one. Luke had more cigarettes. Bryce had more moonshine and could make more when he ran out. We weren't wasting something irreplaceable. Just personal. I closed my book and held it over the railing and let it go. I watched it fall and fall and fall until it finally landed on the highway. "For the road," I said.

Our sacrifices were important to each of us, yet they didn't break us. It wasn't who we were. It was only a part of who we were. We were still the same. The glass of Bryce's jar could never be mended and filled again. The tobacco in Luke's cigarettes would scatter and could never be smoked. The pages of my book would come loose from the binding and be carried away by the wind. The pages and notes could still be read if they were found, but nobody would be able to make sense of the story. They would never feel the meaning the way I did.

We were the same way. We left the only place we ever called home. We jumped off the overpass ourselves to an unknown fate. We were still made up of the same physical matter, but we were shaped differently. Maybe we could never make sense of ourselves and our choices. There was no going back to pick up our pieces.

Bryce kind of ruined the moment, but what could you expect. Moments like that are rare and they are short-lived. "We should go do something totally random. Something we would never have the chance to at home."

"Like what?" Luke asked.

"I have no fucking idea and that's my fucking point. I'm sick of always knowing what I'm gonna do next, ya know? What's the point of life if you can't fuck up with a bad decision every now and then? My entire life has been a bad decision up to this point."

"Good point," I said. "Not that I'm agreeing with that last part."

"Nah, you can agree," Bryce said.

I had to laugh at that a little bit. At least he was honest.

So we took our bags and walked back into the heart of the city. We were all too young to get into the thousands of casinos or bars or anything. So that was unfortunately out of the question. There was so much to do in Vegas but not if you were under twenty-one.

We kept walking and talking for a while, pointing out different things we could do. I suggested that we hit up the Las Vegas Museum of Natural History in the morning. Luke and Bryce looked at me like I was stupid.

"We did not come all this way so we could learn about old shit, dude. If we wanted that, we wouldn't have lied about college," Bryce said.

"Eh, it was worth the shot." I didn't expect anything else.

In a quieter part of the city, we came across this theatre that seemed intriguing enough for us. The sign was lit up and said THE LOST VEGAS BURLESQUE: 21 AND OVER.

"It's Vegas," Luke said. "People here may have low standards and hopefully not card us."

"Looks kind of ghetto," I said. "We can probably manage to get our way in."

Bryce opened the red double-doors and we expected a ticket booth or something, but there wasn't. "Five bucks," this girl said, like she hated her job. She was loudly smacking her gum and her eyeliner was very excessive. She might have had some potential to be pretty, but I couldn't tell. We each handed her a five and she said,

"Thanks. Theatre four. Just sit wherever you find an open seat."

"That was a lot easier than it should have been," Bryce said.

Luke sighed with disappointment. "I was hoping it was going to be harder than that."

I nodded in agreement. "She doesn't even look twenty-one, to be honest."

"Like I said, low standards." Luke was very right.

The theatre was dimly lit except for a few lights that made the stage glow an eerie red. There were maybe thirty or forty people scattered around, mostly within the first five rows. "There's quite a bit of room in the front row," I said. If we were gonna do this, I thought we might as well have gone all the way.

"Okay," Bryce said. "This should be fun. What the hell is burlesque anyway?"

"Not sure. Ask the nerd," Luke said.

"Nerd?" Bryce asked, implying that I should answer. I didn't really let it bother me anymore.

"Just like a bunch of skits or whatever, but, like, more mature. Hence the having to be twenty-one or over."

"Is it a porn play?" Bryce asked.

"Umm, I hope not?" I sort of asked back. "That doesn't really seem like something I would be into."

He and Luke just laughed a little. None of us had any idea what to expect. A few more people filed in over the next fifteen minutes.

We small-talked for a little bit, as was everyone else. I wondered why nobody else was sitting in the front row. I hoped that it wasn't supposed to be reserved or anything.

The red lights changed suddenly to white and the room grew immediately silent. Then a disembodied girl's voice began to talk/sing.

> *You heard that Vegas is just drugs and sex.*
> *But you've never seen the Lost Burlesque.*

I got the idea that most of these people actually *had* seen it when the audience started to sing along with the next couplet thing or whatever.

> *You know Scarlet and Ginger and Johnny the Queen,*
> *But they better move over for Riley King.*

I was kinda weirded out by the fact that Johnny was a queen for some reason, but maybe that was the point. The heavy stage curtains drew back and the stage lights turned off. The entire theatre was black and the people who were apparently regulars whistled and shouted like we were at some rock concert, which I was fairly sure wasn't the case.

A figure walked onstage and then the red lights turned on again, revealing a girl who didn't even look like she was twenty-one, either. "You guys better bow for the king!" she shouted.

Three other people walked out. I was assuming they were Scarlet, Ginger, and Johnny the Queen, who was a tall, skinny dude doused in glitter and wearing a costume that more or less a skimpy robe of red velvet and gold sequins. The three of them literally bowed on their knees in front of Riley King. Johnny held a bejeweled crown above his head. "All hail the sexy Riley King!" There were more shouts from the audience.

Riley took the crown and placed it gently on her head and tore off her robe that was the same as Johnny's. She wasn't, like, naked or anything, but it still wasn't what I expected. She was wearing this red bikini top and a very short skirt made entirely of black feathers. She was beautiful and probably not even nineteen.

I didn't like to call girls hot. I mean, what's up with that? If the world were blind, then maybe it would make sense to call people hot. Like, "Hey blind girl with the pretty voice, may I touch your feet so I know whether or not they're cold? I hate cold feet in bed and if you have cold feet, you have to wear socks when we cuddle or ya know, we can't go out. So, yeah." And if when he touches her feet they happen to be warm, he can call her hot and they can live happily ever after. I know it's stupid, but it makes a bit more sense to me.

Anyway, Riley kinda danced around Johnny like he was a stripper pole for a little bit while he made various remarks about her royal hotness. But I'm pretty sure he's gay, so he wasn't turned on by her at all. She walked away from him and stood near the edge of the stage. "Are you guys thirsty?" Riley asked.

"THIRSTY FOR YOU!" a few guys shouted.

"Ginger, go give our people some drinks," she said.

"Yes, your sexiness," she said, as if she were totally okay with it.

I heard Bryce whisper, "Guys, this is so fucking hot. Weird, but hot."

She went backstage and came out through a door holding a stack of red Solo cups. Johnny and Scarlet came behind her and poured slightly warm beer into everybody's cups. They met Riley back on the stage and dumped a shitload of beer on her head. It ran down her body, dripping from her hair and soaking the feathers of her skirt. Johnny and Scarlet licked the beer from her body, which brought about more shouts from the guys in the audience, including Luke and Bryce. I just couldn't get over the fact of how perfect that girl's face was. She had the most beautiful red hair, but didn't have all the freckles that usually come with it. The paleness of her skin made everything stand out more. Her eyes were a brilliant shade of blue, not the usual green. Everything about her was absolutely flawless. I couldn't take my eyes off of her, and not even in a lustful way, either. She was just remarkable. Sort of like a painting that must have taken years to perfect.

Johnny the Queen started to strip and he was directly in front of me, wearing only his crown and feathery underwear things. I laughed with everybody else when he looked at me, winked, and started dancing. He probably loved the fact that I was just as scrawny and awkwardly tall as he was, but for him, I was unfortunately very not gay. And he was very, very gay. He pulled a small bag from under his crown and poured the contents into his palm. He knelt down on the stage directly in front of me and blew a ton of glitter all over me. "Let's get this little cutie up here!" he said.

I had no idea how I was supposed to react to that. "Uh, that's okay. Maybe someone else," I said, trying to wipe the glitter from my lips.

"It must be you," he said. "You've already been sparkled."

It was then I realized why nobody else sat in the front row.

I stood up from my seat and Johnny just picked me up and pulled me on the stage beside him. "You're so hot!" Bryce shouted.

"Fuck you!" I shouted back.

Luke looked right at me and said, "Dude, take your shirt off."

"What a lovely idea!" Johnny said. "Riley, would you like to do the honors?"

No, please fucking no," I thought. *Anyone but her.* If she saw my skinny-self up close, I'd never have a chance. Not that someone as nerdy as me would ever have a shot with a girl like her anyway. She grabbed the hem of my shirt and whispered, "You're doing so awesome. Just go with it and I'll buy you a drink later." I just nodded. She pulled off my shirt to display to these burlesque-goers that I was very unsexy. "What's your name?" she asked so everyone could here.

"Uh, Wade Larson."

Riley rolled her eyes. "Middle name?"

"It's Duke," I said.

"Parents always give us better middle names than actual names." Riley turned me toward the audience and shouted, "Give it up for the Duke of Vegas!" My name sounded so much cooler when she said it. Like, I was always kinda embarrassed by my middle name, but it made for a decent stage-name, I had to admit. The audience cheered my name over and over again: "Duke, Duke, Duke!" I liked it. Even Luke and Bryce were saying it. I laughed and smiled uncontrollably and I probably looked like a total sparkly, dorky mess up there, but I didn't care. It was finally my moment. A moment that wasn't just praise from teachers and principals. Burlesquing with the beautiful King and the incredibly gay Queen felt so much better than just being good at something I didn't have to work for.

Johnny threw more glitter on me and I bowed again.

All of the people I didn't know continued to cheer my name.

The King held my hand and raised it in the air. "All hail the Duke!"

I had never felt my heart beat so fast.

CHAPTER FOURTEEN

"Can I please have my shirt back?" I asked backstage when the show was over. It was a little over an hour long, and as soon as it was over, the rush was gone, along with my newfound and short-lived confidence.

Riley held my shirt and waved it in front of me. "You can have it back as long as you promise you won't put it back on."

I looked down at my chest. I was covered in glitter and beer and a little bit of lipstick from one of Scarlet's and Ginger's skirt. "I'm a scrawny mess who really should wear a shirt."

"And I am an underage burlesque star who performs illegally to pay the bills. Welcome to Vegas. Nobody is gonna give you a second glance. Trust me, dude."

I sighed. "Okay, fine. But kind of have to go. My friends are probably waiting for me outside. I can't really leave them hanging."

"You can't leave yet. I owe you a drink, remember?" she said.

"Oh! Can I come with you guys?" Johnny asked. He sounded enthusiastic enough for the three of us.

"Jesus, no. I am trying to entertain our new member of the royal family. Just go home and I'll see you next week. Maybe earlier if you're lucky.

Make sure you give Will a big kiss for me, would you, darling?"

"Fine," he said. "But we will go out eventually. It has been much too long, you know." Johnny the Queen left the theatre wearing only his underwear and crown. And that apparently was totally acceptable.

"I wouldn't have cared if he came with us, really," I said.

"I know. Because you're not from here and you don't know how to be anything but nice. But here, nice doesn't cut it."

"How can you tell I don't live here?" I didn't want to think I looked that obviously helpless. You can't take the redneck out of the boy, I suppose.

"You just look lost."

"Tell me about it," I said.

"I can't, because I don't really know you. Anyway, he lives with his gay boyfriend, William. If Johnny's ever sick or too drunk to perform with us, which is more often than you might think, William steps up. They're both cool. But even though they've lived in Vegas their entire lives, they still don't know how to be anything but nice. I think it's just what happens when you're that level of gay. But in spite of that, they make it okay."

"Oh, okay," I said, not really sure of what else to say to that.

"Oh my God, you're not gay, are you?" she said apologetically. "I didn't mean that to be offensive or anything. If you are, that's super cool."

"No, not even a little. I like girls. I, um, don't mean like *lots* of girls or anything. Just that I like them in general, I guess. I've never had a girlfriend or anything. But yeah. Girls are cool." I was not the smoothest guy in the world, okay?

"You shouldn't say that. I know you didn't mean to sound like a pedophile, but you really sounded like a creeper just then. If you're not gay you should proudly proclaim that you love sexy ladies or some shit like that."

"Oh. Well, I just try to be respectful," I said. "Just my southern manners, I'm sure."

"You're so cute, you know that?" She flashed her flawless smile at me. "You don't really come by manners here too often, if at all."

"Um, no. Not really." I didn't wanna be called cute. Girls think kittens and clothes and babies are cute. I wanted her to at least think I was handsome something. I knew I wasn't remotely attractive, but still. It wouldn't hurt.

Riley laughed. "Let's get something to drink and maybe sing a little drunken karaoke back at my place. How's that sound?"

"Do you drink moonshine?" I asked her.

"I've never actually tried it, considering it's, like, illegal to make."

Because she *totally* seemed like the type of person who would care about that.

"Well, my friend Bryce makes it and we have a ton of it in our van. We could get some if you want. He won't care."

"Uh, sure. Yeah. Let's go get some fucking moonshine!" she said. She pulled a red shirt that said *The Killers* over her bikini top and that was it.

Luke and Bryce were back at the ticket stand, trying to attempt to flirt with the girl who sold us our tickets. She looked so unamused.

I introduced Riley to the guys, and the other girl took off right away. I didn't really blame her. "Sorry to interrupt you guys. This is Riley King, the really pretty girl who got soaked in beer," I said.

"Is that your real name?" Luke asked.

"Yup."

"It's a badass name," Bryce said.

"Aww, thanks." She smiled. "What are you names?" I felt jealousy for some reason. I don't know why. It was like I wanted her smile to be only mine.

"Bryce, the guy who drinks a lot."

And then Luke introduced himself as the one who smokes a lot. Those two had no shame.

"I smoke, too. It's the most goddamn disgusting thing ever, but I do," Riley said.

"I totally feel you," Luke said.

"I know you know my name, but to make it official and a little less weird, I'm Wade, the guy who reads a lot and performs impromptu burlesque on the side instead of going to a really awesome college," I said. "In other words, the ultimate maker of poor life choices."

"I feel like I already know you so well," Riley said, laughing.

"And I, you," I said. "So, in recompense for my humiliation, Riley has promised an evening of karaoke and drinking for her and I. Bryce, I was wondering if we can we have some shine? Just, like, four jars of it."

Luke laughed or coughed or something and said, "Who the hell says 'in recompense'"?

"Shut up," I said. "There's nothing wrong with being proper sometimes."

"What's in it for me?" Bryce asked. He just couldn't help a brother out on his own.

"Umm, the fact that you and Luke can sleep in the van without nerdy comments every thirty seconds. And if you feel like making stupid decisions, I won't be there to stop you?"

"Sounds good enough," Luke said.

"Yeah, I guess so," Bryce said. He held out his backpack. "There's only three left in here, but I'm positive it will be more than enough to last both of you for a week. One would probably screw you guys up real good. Have at it and don't throw up on the girl."

"*The girl* is right here and her name is Riley," Riley said, annoyed.

"Whatever," Bryce said. "Well, Luke and I are going to take advantage of this time and have a drunkenly gay orgy session at some male stripper bar. I will see you whenever."

I wish I were lying, but Luke literally kissed Bryce on the cheek just then and Bryce kissed Luke on the cheek right back. I knew they weren't gay, so I had no idea what compelled them to do such things. "Let's go, babe," he said and they walked away to what I hoped was not an actual male stripper bar. But when in Rome…

"They're not usually that level of weird," I said.

"It's okay, seriously. I've seen plenty of weird in my life. Ready to go?" she asked.

"Yeah, let's go. I haven't really had any time away from them in a while. It's driving me insane."

"Then call me your sanity."

*   *   *

We went to a part of Vegas that I never even knew existed. Well, I guess I knew that every city had its ghetto places, but I didn't have a reason to go there.

"It's probably not what you're used to, but it's something," Riley said.

"It's completely okay." I didn't want her to be embarrassed by it. "I live in the most redneck trailer park anyone has ever seen."

She grabbed a key from the mailbox and unlocked the door. "This is it. You can just drop your bags anywhere. Doesn't matter."

I sat them down beside the tattered couch. It looked like it had suffered through many years of butts. "Do you live here by yourself?"

"Uh, no. My mom lives here, too. She's asleep though, since she has to work early. Actually, in about an hour."

"Oh, okay."

"Yup."

I was certain that both of us felt the same awkwardness. "So…"

"Oh, right. Sorry. I've never had anyone over except for Johnny, and he's gay. So, it's not like we're tempted to rip off each other's clothes and fuck on the couch, getting turned on by the fact that my mom could catch us at any time." Riley was really the most spontaneous girl I had ever met.

I just kinda laughed nervously. "That's good. I think."

"I guess. But I wasn't implying that I wanted to rip off *your* clothes or anything. It was just an example."

"Yeah, I figured as much."

"Yeah. So, can you sing?"

"I can, but not well. I usually keep my singing contained to the shower or in the car when I'm the only one in it."

"I'm kind of the same way. Though burlesquing has brought me out of my shell a little. Well, more like a lot. But whatever."

"I bet." I really needed better things to say. "I like The Killers, too."

"What? Oh," she said and looked at her shirt. "Yeah, I got it when they were here in Vegas, like, three years ago, when I was fourteen. I had all the band member's signatures on the back, but I accidentally gave them a Crayola marker to use, so it washed out about a week later. I was pretty pissed off, as you can imagine, but it's how life goes."

"Well, maybe you can see them again and bring a Sharpie."

"Yeah, maybe. That'd be really awesome."

"It would be. I'm seventeen, too. Just so you know that I'm not just a very youthful old dude trying to get in your pants or something."

"Good, because I was somewhat worried about that. Also, I'm not wearing pants."

"I'm not trying to get in your feathered skirt thing, either. It looks like it would tickle too much."

"Awesome."

"I'm a virgin, anyway. Like, I wouldn't have the slightest idea about how to make a move."

"Me, too," Riley said. She must have read an expression on my face that I didn't realize I was making because she said, "Don't look too surprised. I'm not a hooker. I do burlesque. There is a big difference, believe it or not. The only person I ever kissed was Johnny. We tried to see if maybe he was a little less gay than he thought. He was actually kinda grossed out by it, thus proving he is the gayest gay guy ever, what with my being beautiful and whatnot."

"Well, it's true."

"That he's very gay or that you think I'm beautiful?" she asked, and shoved my arm playfully.

"Both," I said. I smiled at her, though my teeth probably looked gross from lack of brushing. I was very aware of that. "Do you happen to have a toothbrush I can borrow or have? I don't care either way. I could give you a few dollars for a new one."

"No, it's okay. You can borrow mine. It's the neon green one. The bathroom's down the hall. Second door on the right. My mom's room is right beside it, so try not to be too loud."

"I promise I'm not going in there to shoot up and make orgasmic sounds at the relief of heroine finally making me feel alive again."

"I'll take your word for it, but if you do, don't make a mess, and don't in my house. That'd be really weird to have to explain to my mom," Riley said. "My room's across from the bathroom, so I'll be listening."

"That makes me rather nervous," I laughed.

"I'm good at that."

"You can take the shine in your room, if you want. Just don't start without me."

"Don't worry. I don't even know if I'm looking forward to it or not."

"Oh."

"I meant the moonshine, not hanging out with you."

"Okay, good," I said, and went into the bathroom to find her toothbrush. I wouldn't even use my dad's toothbrush when we went camping once. Just the thought of it grossed me out. But there I was using a random girl's toothbrush that she could have secretly dipped in a drug earlier in an attempt to steal my wallet. It was odd, but I trusted her.

CHAPTER FIFTEEN

I almost expected Riley to be sitting on her bed wearing some type of lacey lingerie, not to be seductive or anything, but just out of personal preference. But she wasn't. She was wearing baggy gray sweats and a black tank top. Typical girl pajamas, I guess. "I have a confession," she said when I walked in her room.

"*You* were the one shooting up when I was gone?"

"Well, other than that," she said sarcastically.

"Okay?"

"I sniffed the moonshine and I'm kind of afraid to drink it. Like, I only drink the cheap shit they dump on me for the show. I don't even really like beer all that much."

"Yeah, no. No, that's totally fine. I don't really like it either. I just drank some for the first time tonight. I'm not, like, an alcoholic like Bryce is. But he's not a bad guy. He just wants to escape like anybody else." That probably sounded really, really dumb. I mean, if she had tapped into my mind just a few hours before, then she would have understood.

"I know what you mean."

"You do?"

"Of course. Just because I'm not particularly fond of the taste or anything, I like what it does. Well, I don't know. I've seen what it can do to harm people, and in spite of that, I've used it to try to help me forget the harm. It's stupid, I know."

"No, not at all," I said, because it wasn't. It was kind of brilliant actually.

"I would love to go into detail to make me sound like less of a bipolar psycho, but I don't want you to think I want your sympathy, ya know?" Riley said.

"I, uh, yeah, I do. But I know you wouldn't be doing it for me to feel bad for you. I can tell you're not like that."

"Thanks. I guess that's a good thing.'"

"I think so."

"Yeah. Well, for the sake of forgetting the harm of alcohol, let's do it. By it I mean drinking this shit that will probably make us throw up our organs and drowning out the puking with the worst karaoke you will ever hear or perform in your life. Guaranteed." She had this little grin at the left side of her mouth the entire time she spoke and I loved it.

"That sounds very scary and very fun at the same time," I said. I grabbed a jar of moonshine. "Want the first drink?"

"Are you kidding me? I totally have to see your reaction first. I mean, it's not going to influence whether or not I drink it. I just wanna see it actually happen."

"You, my dear, are terrible," I said, laughing.

"Every kingdom needs its crooked king," she said.

"Maybe you're right." I unscrewed the lid from the jar and drank. It didn't go down any easier than it did the first time. I thought I'd just mess with her for a little bit. "Oh, God. Fuck fuck fuck! It fucking burns," I said and swooned onto her floor as dramatically as I possibly could.

"Oh my God, don't die. Please don't die," she said, running to my side. Riley literally checked the pulse on my wrists and neck. I felt a little bad about it.

I laughed and could not stop laughing for the life of me. She punched my arm rather hard. "I'm sorry," I said, catching my breath. "It was just too good to pass up."

"So, it's not that bad?"

"No, but it's kinda bad. I've had it once and it was just like that. No difference at all," I wasn't trying to scare her. I was trying to prepare her. Yes, it was bad enough to require both mental and physical preparation. I was still trying to decide if it was even worth it.

"Do you think it would be more tolerable if we, like, flavored it?"

"Um, I don't know. I've never really thought about it."

"I think there's some lemonade powder in the kitchen we could try?" she suggested.

"Sure. Why the hell not?" I said. "It can't possibly get worse than it already is."

"I wouldn't know, but I'll trust that. Wait here in case my mom wakes up," she said and left.

I just sat there on the floor with the jar in my hands. I sniffed it again for no reason at all. The burning sensation was still the same, too. I ran my hands over the stained carpet. It was a rusty brown in places, like blood that had been scrubbed and dried and faded over time. Something about it made me want to ask about what she said just minutes before, but I didn't want to hurt her again if anything was already wrong.

I could hear some vague conversation, so I assumed her mom was awake for work. After a few more minutes I heard Riley say, "I love you, too," and she came back with the lemonade mix. "Okay. Mom's gone, so that's good. Will you hand me the shine?"

"Sure," I said and gave it to her.

"How much do you think we should use?"

"I would say probably a lot if you even wanna come close to diluting the taste of the alcohol."

"Well, I don't really want to dilute it completely. Just like maybe to the point of those cheap margaritas that come in a can. You know what I'm talking about?"

"Uh, yeah. I think I've seen those."

"Yeah. I can handle those fairly well, I guess." She poured about half a cup of powder into the jar, screwed on the lid, and shook it gently until it turned into this pale yellowish color. "Do you wanna try it?" Riley asked me.

"Nope," I said. "I tried the real stuff for you. Now it's your turn."

She rolled her eyes. "Fine. I guess that's fair."

"Of course it is."

"God, I can't do this," she said. Normally when people say that, it means they're chickening out. But not Riley. She said it and took the biggest drink I had ever seen anyone take other than Bryce. Then she squealed like a little girl and just said various forms of shit and fuck for a couple minutes.

"So, it didn't just taste like spiked lemonade?" I asked, already aware of the answer.

"Hell no. It tasted like I was dying, if that makes sense? I know it doesn't, but still. I would add more but I think it just made it worse. Your turn."

"Fine," I said. I took a drink just as big as hers. Not because I wanted to, but for the sake of looking like a man. I coughed spasmodically for a few seconds and thought I was gonna puke all over her room, which would have made a very bad impression considering the fact that all she did was cuss a lot.

"Well?" she said.

"You're right. It's a lot worse than just drinking it straight up. I'm going to go pour this down your bathroom sink and I'll be right back." It was a double meaning. I also went to the bathroom to throw up. In one night, though it was a few hours apart, I drank an entire jar of moonshine. I had probably consumed, maybe, two ounces of alcohol in my entire life. But in the course of a night, I drank much more than that. My body and liver were probably freaking out. Riley probably heard me throw up, but whatever. At least my stomach was empty so I could hopefully handle a little more.

"Hey," she said when I came back.

"Hey," I said. "Do you want to take a sip of it again without trying to enhance it?"

"Uh, sure." She took another jar and downed half. Her face had the look of *Oh, God, this is awful,* but she handled it okay.

"Better?" I asked.

"Better." She tossed me a jar. "I think we can handle our own this way," she said and drank the rest of hers.

"Thanks." I took a drink. "Yeah, a lot better," I said and finished the jar without stopping.

"Well, that's all of it."

"Yup."

"I still feel the same," she said.

"I imagine that it kicks in when you least expect it. I've never drank that much in my life."

"I probably have, but considering this stuff was, like, really strong, it was easily more than I've ever had at once."

"Yeah, moonshine sucks," I said.

"But at least it's alcohol. And as disgusting as it is, it usually helps until you do something really stupid.

"Yeah."

"Ready for karaoke?" Riley asked.

"Um, yeah. Sure."

It was seven in the morning and it felt like we were on our millionth song. Riley was a terrible singer but it was wonderful. Another random song came on. "Your turn," she said.

I didn't recognize the melody at all. I paused it. "I don't know this song," I admitted.

"What? It's The Killers. I bet that everyone in the fucking world knows this amazing song!" she yelled.

"I know who it is. I just don't know this particular song."
"It's super easy to learn. I promise." Her words were starting to slur and mine probably were, too. "I'll sing with you," she said. She hit play and together we sang. Her voice was off-key but confident. Mine was barely louder than a mumble, but I was able to get the words out:

It started out with a kiss.
How did it end up like this?
It was only a kiss.
It was only a kiss...

There was nothing and no one in the world but the most beautiful king and I.

CHAPTER SIXTEEN

I heard a woman calling out something and then I noticed a beautiful girl asleep beside me. Then I knew what the voice was saying. "Riley? I'm home."

"Shit," I whispered to myself. "Shit. Riley, wake up. Wake up!" I shook her gently until she groaned and nearly hit me in the face.

"Jesus, what? There is literally no reason in the world I need to be up this early."

"You probably have the most severe hangover in the world right now, but your mom's back."

She sat up quickly then said, "Ow, my head. Too fast." She inhaled sharply. "Okay, I'm good. I feel like I'm gonna throw up my organs, but I'm good. I've been much worse. How do I look?"

"Considering the circumstances, you look amazing." And I meant it.

There was a knock on her bedroom door. "Honey? Are you awake?"

"Oh, hey, Mom. I was just, uh, reading and had my earbuds in. I didn't hear you come home," she said through the door.

"I bought a pizza if you're hungry. Sorry I didn't get a chance to make supper for you."

"Yeah, I'm starving. And it's cool, Mom. I know you're busy. I'll be out in a couple minutes," Riley said, already changing into a pair of jeans. I tried not to watch.

She was a much better liar than I was. Though I didn't take her as the reading type. That could have been the worst lie to tell. I'm not saying she was stupid. I knew how smart she was right away, but more like a thoughtful kind of smart. She had answers for everything.

"Should I, like, attempt to sneak out your window or something?" I asked.

"Uh, no. I think we'll be okay. She trusts me a lot more than most parents do or should trust their teenagers."

"That's good." I wondered how any parent could trust their daughter in Las Vegas. It just seemed like a breeding ground for really poor choices.

"Yeah. She's a pretty awesome mom."

"We should probably brush our teeth or something first. So we don't smell like shine so much. She might freak out a little more then." I knew it wouldn't have gotten rid of the scent completely, but I thought that maybe the smell of mint would lessen the alcohol. Then again, it could have just made us more obvious. I mean, who really sneaks boys into their house and cares enough to brush their teeth in the morning?

"Good idea." She finished getting dressed and then we took turns with her toothbrush and smelled each other's breath. After brushing three times, we decided it was as good as it was going to get.

We walked in the kitchen and her mom was setting two paper plates and two cans of Coke on the table. She looked up and saw Riley and me standing there. "I'm still a virgin," Riley said. She definitely cleared up any confusion there.

"Good to know," her mom said. "Who's your friend?"

"Wade Duke Larson. Also known as the Duke. He's new to Vegas, so I thought he could use someone as street-smart as myself. We did the show together last night."

"Ah. Sounds fun, kiddo. Did Johnny sparkle him?"

"Indeed, he did," she said and laughed.

I wondered if Riley brought home every guy that Johnny sparkled. But then I doubted it. She probably wouldn't have been as nervous were that the case.

"Well, it's nice to meet you, Wade," she said.

"Call him Duke," Riley said. "It'll help build his confidence."

"I am perfectly confident on my own, thank you very much," I said.

"Uh-huh. Sure you are," Riley said. "Don't listen to him, Mom. Country boys don't know anything."

Her mom laughed. "Duke," she corrected herself.

"Nice to meet you, too," I said, and held out my hand out of habit. She didn't seem to think it was weird. She shook it.

"We have plenty of food, if you'd like to stay and eat with us," Riley's mom said.

"Thanks, Miss King," I said.

"You can call me Jen. I'll help you feel confident and you can keep me feeling young. How does that sound?"

"Fair enough," I said.

The pizza was pepperoni, which was something else I knew that I needed to get used to. I ate it without complaint, and it was honestly not bad.

"So, what brought you to Vegas?" Jen asked. "Most people that end up here have some kind of a story to tell."

"Um, a bad decision that actually turned out to be worth it," I said, and smiled at Riley.

"Sounds like the answer quite a few people here would have."

"Well, it was completely unlike me to even think about coming here, but a couple of my friends talked me into it. So, here I am."

"He's handling it really well," Riley said. "He's from a small town in West Virginia that no one's ever heard of." She picked off her pepperoni and put it in a little pile off to the side. I looked at her curiously. "What? It's my favorite part. I always eat it last."

"No, no. It's cool," I said. "Weirdo." I smiled at her.

"Well, you'll love it here, hate it here, or feel like you're stuck here," Jen said.
"Me? I'm just stuck. But it's not too bad these days."

"Mom," Riley said. I knew that tone. That was the voice of, *If you don't stop talking right now, you're really gonna piss me off.*

"Just being honest with him. I don't want you to be stuck here like me and I know absolutely nothing about this boy. For all I know, he could turn out to be just like your father."

I sat there awkwardly and silently, not really sure of what was going on.

"What the hell is wrong with you?"

"Nothing, I just worry about you."

Riley stood up from her chair. "Let's go, Wade."

"It's okay, really. She's just looking out for you."

"No, she isn't. She's just being a bitch," Riley said, as if her mother weren't sitting in the same room. "You know it's not okay. Let's go."

So she and I just walked off, and I was still very much in the dark about whatever it was they were talking about. We wandered through the streets of her neighborhood with no particular destination in mind. I thought of Luke and Bryce and wondered how they were managing in Vegas on their own.

Riley stopped walking in a random alley. She sat on the gravel beside two garbage cans that were swarming with flies. It smelled awful, like rotting leftover meat that had been outside in the heat for a while. I sat down beside her and picked at the pebbles. I didn't touch her or say anything until she finally spoke up.

"I am so, so sorry about that. She's not usually that way, I swear."

"Don't worry about it," I said.

"How can I not worry about it? She basically brought up the whole thing I was trying to avoid telling you."

"You don't have to tell me anything, okay?" I said. I could tell that she seemed jittery. She extended her legs and kept crossing and uncrossing them at her ankles.

"I still don't really know anything."

"If I want to be honest, I have to tell you everything."

"No, you don't, Riley. What happened between you and your mom is none of my business. I hardly even know you. I promise you that it's fine."

"I know you saw the stains on my carpet."

"I don't know that you're talking about," I lied. I didn't want her to feel uncomfortable or like she was obligated to tell me.

"Don't lie to me, Duke. They're impossible to miss. It's blood, if you were wondering." Her voice cracked and her eyes began to fill with tears. "Mine."

"Please don't tell me this. It's hurting you too much. We can just let it go." She looked so sad. I felt terrible because I thought it was my fault.

"You can let it go because you never had to deal with it to begin with. When I was fourteen, the same year as the concert, my dad left my mom and me. He, uh, he just told my mom he couldn't do it anymore. He came in my room that night. I pretended to be asleep and he didn't bother to wake me up. He just kissed the top of my head and that motherfucker had the nerve to whisper that he loved me very much. I knew that he and my mom were having problems. I heard them fight all the time. And I still loved him. But that was the night I really learned what it was to hate. I could smell the bourbon on his breath."

I touched her hand that was resting on her lap. It was shaking.

"I was so pissed off at him. I was pissed at my mom for a while to. I would yell at her and ask her why she let him leave and what she did to make him go. She said she didn't know, over and over again. But I didn't believe her. I knew she did something. Then maybe a couple months after my dad left, I went in my room."

"Riley, just stop. Please." I couldn't stand to watch her cry. "Please," I whispered.

But she kept going. "I locked the door. My mom was in the shower so I knew she wouldn't hear me if I screamed or cried. I didn't know what would happen. My dad didn't take anything with him when he left, so I snuck into my parent's room one night and stole his pocket knife. I sat on the floor where you and I slept last night and I took out the knife." She stopped and laughed, but nothing funny was happening. Sometimes people laugh even when they're in pain. It's just something to hide behind. It's the saddest thing.

"Anyway," she said. "I rolled up the sleeves of my shirt just enough so that my wrists were visible. I was fucking fourteen years old. I barely lived. It was too young to wanna die. But I didn't think about how fucked up it was in the moment. I cut my wrists. It wasn't deep at first. Just little scratches on my skin. I could feel the sting, almost like a paper cut." She showed me her wrists then. I could see so many scars that I never would have noticed. "But it didn't help. I was still alive and I didn't want to be. And if you don't have to live, why do it if you don't want to? I cut deeper until I hit a vein. There was so much blood and I got scared. It was only the blood that scared me, not the thought of dying. It was pretty fucked up. I screamed for my mom, for my dad, for anybody. It wouldn't stop bleeding." She closed her eyes, like she was trying so hard to remember every detail.

"I could feel life just fading away, and I was happy in the wierdest way. I wouldn't have to feel anymore. My mom came running with just a towel on. She couldn't open the door. She called 911 when I wouldn't answer. I guess I lost too much blood, so I passed out. Paramedics broke down my door and they carried me away. I was falling in and out of consciousness the entire time, so I remember the little things. My mom told me a lot of it."

"I'm so sorry, Riley," I said. I held her and she just started crying uncontrollably on my shoulder. Saying sorry couldn't do anything to heal that kind of pain, I knew. But I just couldn't sit there and not say anything. I rubbed up and down her back.

She pulled away a little, so I let her go. She wiped the tears from her face and her red eyes. "They watched me in the hospital for a while. I wasn't allowed to go back home for three months so they could monitor my behavior or whatever. They made me talk to a therapist about my dad, but it didn't help. People should have friends to go to for shit like that, you know? Therapists are just for people with problems that don't have friends. People like me, I guess."

"Yeah, I know what you mean. We shouldn't be forced to tell strangers what's wrong."

"Exactly," she said. She was still sniffling and wiping snot from her nose, but the tears stopped falling. "When they finally let me go back home, I could tell that my mom tried to clean up the blood in my carpet so I wouldn't have to remember it every single day for the rest of forever. The stains were still there all over the place. I didn't really realize how bad it actually was until I saw the stains. But I never said anything to my mom. She never said anything to me. Neither of us really brought it up again. I know she still worries, though. I'm not allowed to lock my door anymore, but if it's closed she'll always knock first. It took a long time for her to trust me enough to go back to work again without being afraid that I'll off myself when she's gone. I mean, I've thought about it plenty of times, but I never do anything."

"So, are you doing better now?" I asked.

"I wouldn't say that I'm ever really okay, but I'm a little better. It's been three years."

"That's good."

"Yeah," she said.

"I won't be like your dad."

"I know."

"I won't leave you like that."

"Okay."

I hugged her again and held her. We stayed there like that for a while without saying anything. Yet nothing was left unsaid in that moment.

CHAPTER SEVENTEEN

"Thanks for not thinking that I'm, like, some terrible person or anything," Riley said. We were walking around again. Home was the last place she wanted to be. As for me, I didn't think I even had one anymore.

"I would never think that about you. You are a person who went through a bad thing, but that's not who you are. We are not the things we face. We just find ourselves later on because of it." I don't even think I knew what I was talking about. All I knew was that I needed to be there for her.

"Yeah, I guess that could be true. I don't want you to think I'm like an attention whore. I'm totally not. It's just—I don't know. I feel like I can be open with you. It's stupid because I don't even know you. But whatever. It's done," Riley said.

My phone rang at the most inconvenient time. "It's the one who smokes a lot," I said.

"You can get that," she said.

"Thanks." I answered the phone.

Me: You're on speaker, man.

Luke: Yeah, so are you.

Me: Okay. So, what's up with you guys?

Bryce: Are you with that hot chick?

Riley: Again, my name is Riley. And yes, I'm with him.

Bryce: Feisty. I like it.

Me: Shut the fuck up.

Riley: How were the gay men?

Luke: Attractive.

Me: Wait, what? Did you seriously go?

Luke: We did.

Bryce: They offered Luke a job. They said I was a little too chubby for what they were looking for, those pretentious bastards.

Me: Don't they know you're underage?

Luke: Yeah, but they don't really care. I'm pretty sure that nobody here really give a shit about anything. I think I'm gonna do it.

Me: Good luck with that.

Luke: Thanks.

Bryce: So, when are you meeting up with us?

I looked at Riley and she smiled that crooked grin that I loved.

Me: Uh, I have no idea.

Luke: Did you fuck her?

Riley: I'm still *right here*.

Me: No, I didn't fuck her. We're just hanging out.

Bryce: Whatever, dude. Anyway, Luke and I gonna take off. You do your thing and we can do ours. Looks like this trip did you some good after all, didn't it?

Me: Yeah. I hate to admit it, but I am really glad I listened to you and Luke.

Luke: I told you that you weren't always right.

Me: I know. I just didn't like admitting it much.

Luke: Or at all, really.

Bryce: Take care of yourself, man. We're gonna go find us some ladies or some shit.

Me: Don't drink too much.

Bryce: Ha! You're funny, dude. Later.

I hung up the phone and put it back into my pocket.

"You really could use better friends," Riley said. "They're kind of douchebags."

"I know. But they used to be the only ones who would ever talk to me. I did their homework for them throughout much of middle school and high school. I'm sure that helped."

She laughed. "Yeah, I bet it did. I didn't really care enough about school to even have someone do shit for me. I am completely hopeless."

"Oh, I don't think I would go that far," I said.

"So, what are you gonna do now?"

"I don't know. It's Vegas. There's everything to do."

"Are you hungry?" she asked. "I know we didn't really get the chance to eat much. I'll have to apologize to my mom about that. And I'll make sure she apologizes to you, too."

"It's okay."

"Stop being so nice. That'll only get you ripped off here." She condescendingly patted my back. "You'll get there one day, kid."

"Good to know. Maybe Luke landed a job as a gay stripper with his doucheness, which I realize isn't even a real word, but I don't give a fuck."

"Living on the edge, aren't you? That's probably the case. Luke's not that attractive at all. Or at least not my particular type. Anyway, you never answered my question."

"Which one?"

"Are you hungry?"

"Oh, um, yeah. If you are."

"I never get why people say that, as if whether or not I'm hungry is the deciding factor about whether your body needs food or not. Lucky for you, I am very starving."

"Yeah. Lucky me," I said.

"Right. Do you like hotdogs?" Riley asked.

"Um, I guess?" I didn't tell her that I only recently decided to eat certain foods like pepperoni and Skittles but always ate hot dogs, which were probably even more artificial than pepperoni flavored Skittles would be. I really didn't understand my own logic behind it.

"Awesome. Because if you didn't, I'd still take you to the same place."

"I am *honored* to have such a strong say in things."

"You're not even gonna ask me where?"

"Fine. Where are you taking me?"

"Vegas Dawgs. Not spelled like the animal."

"So, spelled in the way someone might say, 'Yo, Waddup, dawg?'"

Riley rolled her eyes but her smile lingered. It was always there at least a little bit. "Promise me you'll never say that again. But yes, that was the appropriate context."

I tried not to smile. I knew my eyes would give it away, though. "I promise. And so I assumed."

"Keep one thing in mind," she said.

I wasn't sure what I needed to keep in mind about a hotdog restaurant unless they were ran by religious people and we couldn't talk about gays, including stories about Johnny. So, I just nodded.

"Their service can be super annoying. All the guys, women are included in that category, wear their pants really, really low and they talk to you as if you are their thug or bro person. You just have to go with it. In spite of how much I dislike the environment, they do have the best hotdogs ever. Like this particular restaurant has five stars in a bunch of Vegas tourism shit. You'll like it."

That particular description of Vegas Dawgs creeped me out a little, but if it had five stars, how bad could it really have been? Though I wasn't sure there were many hotdog-only restaurants to compare it to. I'm just used to the gas station hot dogs, about which I never had a single complaint (except for the occasional stale bun and low ketchup supplies). "Sounds good," I said, not wanting to verbalize my every thought, lest she think of me as odd or something, which would not be inaccurate. But still.

*   *   *

"Yo! How's it going, dawgs," a tall, skinny guy said as soon as we walked into the restaurant. Riley was not wrong about a single description.

"I'm doing okay," I said.

"Just okay?" the guy asked, his pitch suddenly higher. "You're in Sin City, man. You got yourself a pretty girl. You can do any fucking thing you want and get away with it!"

"Carl, language!" a lady yelled from somewhere. I couldn't see her.

"Yes, ma'am," Carl said. "My boss," he whispered to Riley and me.

"Ah, those are never fun," I said.

"You got that right, son. Table or booth for you two?" he asked.

"One of life's greatest and most puzzling philosophical questions," Riley said and looked at me, wanting my opinion.

"Um, booth?" I asked.

"Sure," Carl said and grabbed two menus. "Follow me." So we did. All of the booths turned out to be taken. "I am so sorry about that. Do y'all wanna wait or is a table good instead?"

"That's fine," Riley said, again looking at me for approval. I nodded.

But Carl gave us the worst frickin' table in the entire history of bad tables. It was right in the center of everything and everyone. I wasn't paranoid or so self-centered to think everyone would stare at us. I just don't like being in the center of things. Well, that's not true. I like being the smart kid that everyone knows is smart and hates for being the teacher's pet. But I was working on that. I really was. It's just that I don't really have any good traits. If I'm going to be appreciated, it has to be for something I'm good at.

"What can I get you to drink?" he asked, breaking through my conceited mental ramblings.

"Chocolate milk, please," I said.

"Uh, root beer. Thank you," Riley said.

"Be right back," Carl said and walked off somewhat crookedly as he tried to keep his pants up.

Riley was just kinda looking at me. But not casually glancing or anything. Like really looking. The kind of looking that violates the privacy of your soul. It made me uncomfortable, so I flipped through the menu. I tried to say something that wouldn't lead to deep conversation. Riley was smart. The thoughtful kind of smart. She was the kind that could help people. I was smart for my own merit, and that's it. "Never in my life have I seen so many ways that a hotdog can be prepared." And it was true. There was the traditional shit like Chili Dawgs and Ballpark Hotdawgs. Then there were things I was scared to try like the China Dawg and the Junkyard Dawg, which I guess just came with literally anything you wanted. But there was a max of ten toppings. I assumed it would have been served with a fork.

"I know, right? But I just get the Chili Dawg every time. A few of the things weird me out. The Chili Dawg is a safe way to go."

"I think I'll just get a hotdog with extra ketchup."

"Also a safe way to go, Duke."

"Yeah, I figured. Like what the hell is a China Dawg?"

"Oh, I asked about that once. They said it's basically like a hotdog eggroll."

"That sounds really terrible," I said.

"I agree. I haven't asked about anything else since. I don't even open the menu."

Carl came out with our drinks then. He set them down on the table. "Are you ready to order or do you need a few more minutes?"

"I think we're ready," Riley said. "I'll have the Chili Dawg with cheese and extra onions, please. And a side of fries."

I closed my menu. "I will have, uh, just a hotdog with extra ketchup. And fries, too."

"Okay," he said. "We'll get that right out to you in a few." And he walked off, checking on other tables.

Carl gave us our food fifteen minutes later. I grabbed a fry and put it in my mouth right away. It wasn't worth it. It just really burned my tongue. I blew on the next few, dipping some in the ketchup on my hotdog.

Riley wasn't shy about eating like a lot of girls are. She ate with her hands, not a fork, and when chili dripped on her shirt, she said fuck and moved on with her life instead of whining about how it was her favorite shirt, though it wasn't really, and wiping at the stain for ten minutes, rubbing it in deeper rather than cleaning it.

"This is really good," I said. "Better than the gas station hot dogs I'm used to back home."

"I told you," she said with her mouth full. "So, Duke, I feel like we don't know much about each other. Well, you know more about me than I know about you. What's your story?"

I distractedly played with the fries on my plate. "What?"

"Your story. You know, why you're here?"

"I told your mom earlier, remember?" I said.

Riley leaned forward in her seat. "That was not a story. It was a summary of a summary. There is no way your life is that boring."

"Uh, it's nothing exciting. Luke and Bryce convinced me to not go to college. Now here I am."

"Which school were you supposed to go to?"

"Harvard."

She looked completely shocked. I pulled out my phone and took a picture because her expression was just that priceless. "No shit. You were accepted?" No response to the taking of the picture.

"Yup."

"You're one of those rich kids, aren't you?"

"No, not really. Average."

"Whatever. Keep going," she said.

"Okay, well I obviously agreed to the plan and my parents don't know. They think I'm getting a good education in New England and dating a future lawyer, not eating hotdogs with a beautiful burlesque performer in Las Vegas."

"Do you regret not going to school? That was clearly the safer option."

"Why do you ask?"

She just sighed. "I don't know. I mean, you just seem like you have a lot of potential to do great things with your life."

"See, I was always thinking about that. I always wanted to be famous for some great, unwritten masterpiece that I would be the one to write. I got tired of mattering widely being my only reason for living. It took two of the biggest idiots I've ever met to get me to see that."

"But do you regret it?"

I paused and looked at her in the way that maybe violated her soul, too. "Not at all." All she did was smile in a way that I've never seen from her.

"What?" I asked.

"Nothing," she said and ate a few of her fries.

"Did you mean that?"

I was confused. "Regarding?"

"When you said I was beautiful."

"You're very beautiful," I said without hesitation.

"You're not too bad yourself," she said, still smiling.

"Um, thank you, I think?"

"I think you're welcome." She looked so amazing. I memorized all of her. The different shades in her eyes. The brilliant orange of her hair. That crooked smile that never left. "You're staring," she said.

"Oh, sorry."

"It's okay. I think I was staring at you earlier."

"Only a little bit," I said.

She didn't say anything. All we did was stare at each other for the longest time. It wasn't even really awkward or anything. I don't know how to accurately describe it. Carl interrupted us at some point. "Are you ready for the check?"

"Sure," Riley said, not looking away from me.

Carl walked away and we continued in our silence. I leaned forward, held her face in one of my hands, and tried to kiss her. She pulled away. "I'm sorry," I said, feeling like a douchebag for just assuming she would be okay with it.

"No no no. It's not you. It's just, hold on." She dug around in her purse for a minute. "Jesus," she said. I sat there quietly, unsure of what was going on. Then out of nowhere she just stood up and shouted "Does anybody have a stick of gum?!" There was a young couple sitting a few tables away from us. The lady walked up and handed a piece to Riley. The two of them exchanged a few quiet words. I could only make a few certain words, but there was definitely something about onions and a kiss. "You are a lifesaver," I heard Riley say.

She sat back down across from me and made a dramatic scene of opening the piece of gum. It was light green, so it figured it was spearmint. Strong enough to cover a bit of onion breath. She put it in her mouth and chewed it exactly ten times. I counted. Then she leaned forward over the table and kissed me. It was kind of more passionate than what I was gonna try for, but I didn't object. I just fell into it. I felt her lips part and I could taste the fresh mint on her breath. There was a hint of onion, but I didn't care. I didn't care about anything but Riley and that moment. A few seconds later she pulled away and leaned back in her chair, exhaling. "Wow. Okay."

Those were a couple of my thoughts, too. "I love you, Riley King."

"What?" She seemed shocked and confused.

"I love you."

"No, you don't."

"I do."

"How do you know? I'll just be a waste of your time, Wade. I come with too many problems and too much bullshit you don't need."

"I don't care, Riley. I don't. You're really amazing. I'm not just saying that because that kiss was amazing, and it was, but because you are a great person. You don't come with bullshit. Okay? You dealt with more than you deserve, and I'm sorry. But I love you." I wasn't normally that straightforward, but everything I said was true. There is nothing that should be said more openly and more easily than the truth.

"You can do so much better than me. I'll just do burlesque shows until I'm too old to be called beautiful and I'll live like everyone else, unextraordinary and unremarkable. You are so smart, Duke. You're brilliant. I'm nothing," she said. Her eyes were turning red and I could see the tears welling up. But she fought it and tried to keep that smile on the corner of her mouth, though I could see how broken she was. How little she thought of herself.

"Riley, you will always be beautiful. Your eyes will never lose that happy

177

sparkle, even when you're sad." I reached across the table and wiped away a tear that had finally fallen to her cheek. "You are beautiful now and forever. Your mind is beautiful. Your heart is timeless. You are so smart and you don't even realize how fantastic you are. I love you and everything about you." Then she really started crying. "Hey. Look at me." I tilted her chin upward and locked our eyes. "It'll be okay. All right?"

She nodded. "Okay."

"Thank you."

"For what?"

"Listening to me and believing me."

"I love you, too."

I kissed her this time, and successfully. "I've been trying so hard to matter. I have been searching for meaning. You are it."

She dabbed at her eyes with a greasy napkin she wiped her hands on. "Let's get out of here."

CHAPTER EIGHTEEN

Riley and I left Vegas Dawgs and she asked me sort of an unexpected question.

"Have you ever been to a cemetery?"

"Uh, yeah. Once. When my grandma died."

"Did you ever look at random graves and think?"

"No?" I didn't know that there was anything to really think about dead people I didn't know.

"Let's go the LVC." I found out later that it simply stood for the Las Vegas Cemetery, but people just call it the LVC. It sounded more like some dance club to me than a cemetery when put that way. I guess Vegas citizens wanted to sound trendy even in death.

"Okay."

"Please don't think I'm weird. I mean, weirder than you already anticipated," Riley said.

I laughed. "Oh, you don't have to worry about that. I love *you*, not just normal you, but weird you, drunk you, sad you, silly you. Even pissed off you when I screw up, because we both know it'll happen. I just love you. Who wants normal anyway? Normal people scare me." I don't think I had said love that many times in my life. I didn't know if it was possible that I *really* loved her after so little time together, but I sure felt like I did.

That brought a laugh out of her. "Good point. And I love weird you, too. And all the different kinds of you. Even the ones I don't know yet."

"We'll make a great team," I said.

"Definitely. I hope you have your walking shoes on. It'll be, like, a thirty-minute walk at least." I looked down at my feet. I was wearing converse. Both of us were, actually.

"Yeah, I'm good."

"Awesome. Let's go," Riley said.

She didn't say anything after that for a while. Neither of us did. We just walked to the cemetery in dead silence, as if we were part of a procession. I was almost kinda grateful when my phone rang. It was my mom. "I have to get this," I said.

"No problem."

Me: Hey, Mama.

Mom: Hi, Wade. How are you doing? It's been a while.

Me: Just busy, that's all. Sorry I haven't called.

Mom: It's fine, son. So, how's school? Have your eye on any girls?

Me: Um, yeah. I do, actually. She's great.

Mom: I knew you would! You gotta bring her home one day.

Me: We'll see. Hey, sorry to cut this short, but I have to get to class. I love you. Tell Dad the same.

Mom: I will, honey. I love you, too.

She made a kissing sound into the phone and I hung up.

"Your mom?" Riley asked.

"It was."

"You're a pretty good liar."

"I know. I didn't used to be that way. Is that a bad thing? What if good lying is the precursor for all criminalistic acts? I can't go to jail," I said, being slightly sarcastic. But the jail thing was very true. I was not cut out for that life.

"You're much too sweet to be a criminal," she assured me.

I wrapped my hand around her waist and kissed the top of her head. "I guess you're right."

"Aren't I always?"

"Would saying yes make it easier on me?" I didn't really understand the mind of a girl. It was uncharted territory for me.

"Hmm...maybe," she said rather coyly.

"Then yes." I smiled and she smiled back. God, I loved her so much. All the pain in the world couldn't dim that smile.

"Maybe always has a side of no," Riley pointed out.

"Yeah, but I think I'll take my chances."

The sun was setting by the time we reached the LVC. The gates were still open, chains hanging down on either side. "Isn't that stupid?" Riley asked.

"Is what stupid?"

She pointed to the sign on the gate. "That cemeteries close at dusk. What if the person you loved more than anyone in the world died after dusk and you want to visit them at the time they died every year or month or day or whatever. Cops can't arrest somebody for crying over that grave after dusk. I'm sure so many people have fallen asleep after dusk, exhausted from their broken hearts. A cop would have to have no heart at all to arrest somebody for that. What's the point of cemeteries closing? It's stupid."

I hadn't ever really thought about it like that, but she thinks of everything and she was right. So right. "Yeah, I get what you mean." There is something much more intimate about the night. I've driven past cemeteries before during the day and I've seen a lot of people laying flowers or pictures on the graves of their mothers, fathers, husbands, wives, children who should never have been buried that soon. But it's an open mourning. Darkness can shroud everyone else in the world and make that moment of tears and lost love purely between the dead and the living.

"I probably wouldn't listen to that rule if I had a reason to visit someone," I said.

"A lot of people don't."

"Yeah."

"Let's go in," Riley said. So at dusk, we walked into the cemetery of bodies we didn't even know. Our breathing seemed to quiver for some reason, as if we both felt the heaviness in that moment. There was this small tomb with THE JAMISON FAMILY etched into the gray-black marble. It stood at least ten feet tall. "Pretentious, isn't it?" she said.

I thought about what she meant, and I knew immediately. "Totally. As if the fact that they have a tomb that towers over everyone else makes them better or something."

"But it doesn't."

"Of course not. Because they're all dead. Death is always the same, really. Just this state of no longer being anywhere," I said.

"Can I ask you something?"

"Yeah, sure."

She kinda laughed that nervous laugh. "I just don't want you to think I'm stupid for asking this."

"No, it's okay. I'd never think you're stupid. You're not." I meant it. I was friends with Luke and Bryce for years. I dealt with their shit. Some of the stupidest shit ever said or thought by Riley was not even close to stupid.

"Okay. Well, do you believe in something, ya know, after we die?"

"Like heaven?"

"No. Not necessarily. I mean, heaven only gives hope to Christians, and we're not all Christians, so that's not fair. Like, good people don't always believe in God or Something at all. But they deserve a heaven just as much as anyone else. I find it hard to believe that religious people are the only ones who deserve some form of pure happiness and the rest of us just get damned forever. That's bullshit."

"It is bullshit. I've learned about religions at school and it's total bullshit.

There are thousands of gods and thousands of futures each of the gods lead to. I think if there is a heaven or at least a place better than all this," I said, referring to life in general, I guess, "then everyone should get a shot. We all deal with this fucking life, the good and the bad. I find it very hard to believe that only the few people who believe in the all-powerful creator, God with a capital G, can get there."

"Couldn't have said it better myself," she said. "I think the same thing. Some people even say it's a sin to kill yourself. Can you believe that?"

"Really?" I hadn't heard that. I think she'd thought about life and death and religion more than me.

"Yeah, like if you off yourself, you take away God's ultimate gift so He'll take away your chance of afterlife. But I think the only reason people kill themselves anyway is to get to that happy place faster. Life just becomes too much and it's hard to put up with it. The thought of everything finally being okay is just stronger than the hope of things getting better. You can't damn a person to hell for thinking that."

"That's why I hate religion sometimes. You get all these people telling everyone else what to do and scaring people who don't believe the way they do. Killing yourself is not a sin. Not at all. I think that it's really sad how many people do it, but I think you're right about the reason why they might do it in the first place. It's just another escape for the when the drugs and alcohol become too weak to drown the pain and reality. It's just a permanent escape. I just wish they had more help, you know?"

I was scared that Riley was talking so much about this, considering she had attempted to kill herself when she was younger. I tried to not let it get to me. She was just asking questions about something that bothered her. I didn't understand exactly because I hadn't felt enough pain to want to die the way she did. I just wanted to help her and let her know that she didn't deserve to be damned to hell for wanting to die. Nobody does.

"Thank you," she said.

"You're welcome, but why?"

"For not, like, judging me or thinking that I'm some insane person fucked beyond repair. I just think a lot, I guess. I've never really had anyone to talk about it to. Like, I can't tell things like that to a therapist. Therapists think they help us, but we give them the most shallow information possible. Just enough to get by and enough to make them think they're doing something right. If I tried to talk to my mom like that, she'd think I was on the verge of slitting my wrists again." There it was again. Her nervous laugh. The one that she used to hide something. And that made me nervous, too. Scared, even.

"Are you okay, Riley?" That was the worst possible question I could have asked. What does okay even mean? It is such a misleading word. If people are feeling good and everything is fantastic, they'll say it. We thrive on happiness, so we tend to take even the smallest amount of it and hold on to it as long as we can. And if people are feeling sad and broken, you can see it. Their entire being is just dull, if that makes sense. Okay is for the sad. Okay is for the broken. Okay is for the people who think okay is good enough to get by. But nobody deserves their entire life to be just okay. I regretted asking, so before she answered, I rephrased the question. "I mean, how are you doing? Really. I wanna know." Because she would have said yes. She would have told me that she was okay. Because it doesn't mean much of anything at all.

She shook her head and sat down, her back against the tomb that started all of this. I sat down beside her.

"You can tell me," I said. "You are so important to me, and I want you to be the happiest person alive." I know that sounded really corny, but I wasn't good at relationships considering I never had been in one, let alone being in a relationship with a girl who was so brilliant and so broken. I loved her. I just needed to find some way to help.

"I'll be okay."

And that's when I knew how sad she really was. I held her and rubbed her back. She wasn't even crying. She was just breathing in a way that was so controlled that I knew she was doing everything in her power to not cry. "It's fine to cry, you know," I said.

"I know it is," she said. "But I'm just so tired of doing it. It never helps anymore. It only reminds me of how far-gone I actually am. It sucks so much, Wade."
The sun was gone. The stars were dim because of the haze of the city. I felt her shudder. I pulled her in closer to me.

"Are you cold?"

"No, I'm fine," she whispered.

"Have you ever seen stars without all of the city being in the way?" I asked.

"Uh, not that I remember. I'm used to them being sort of dull."

"Well, you're not missing much. You would drown them out in a heartbeat anyway." Though it was dark, our eyes had adjusted enough. I could see her smile.

"I love you, Duke."

"I love you, King."

"Thank you."

"For?" I asked.

"For loving me first," she said.

"No. I think we loved each other all along. We just had to find each other first."

"Maybe you're right."

"I know that's really hard to admit," I said, and I felt her laugh.

"I had to swallow a lot of pride."

"I bet." I took her hand and held it in mine. The black nail polish was chipped slightly around the edges as if she bit them. I looked at her wrists, and I could just barely see the scars that she really didn't do to herself. I didn't believe that. They were the scars of everything bad in her life. The scars of everything I wanted her to just unexperience and unfeel. I brushed my lips against her papery skin and I kissed the scars that marked her arm. They weren't flaws and I didn't want her to be ashamed of them. Not a single one of them was her fault. "I'm never going to let things be that bad again, okay?"

"Yeah."

"I need you to be here with me forever."

"I promise I'll never leave."

"Don't go."

"I won't," she said.

"Neither will I."

"I believe you."

"Good."

"We should probably go."

"Yeah," I said. "You're mom's probably worried." I stood up and held out my hand so I could help Riley to her feet. "I wouldn't want her to think I eloped with her daughter. I mean, we're in Vegas. There a hundred places to get married really quickly if you felt like it."

I heard Riley laugh. It was a real one.

We walked deeper into the cemetery instead of leaving right away. There were so many children. It was hard to look at them. She and I took turns pointing out names like Lucy-Lynn Lincoln, who sounded like she would have been a pilgrim but just died ten years ago at the age of eighty-two. We imagined lives for the dead just for the fun of it. We spoke of how one day we would be buried here and how years from now a couple of teens would imagine the lives we lived and hoped their musings were as badass as we really were.

At the far end of the cemetery there was a small chapel and beside it lay maybe twenty or so marble headstones. "Don't you just love the idea of unengraved gravestones?" Riley asked.

"Um, I haven't really thought much about it."

"It's just that all of us, the second we are born, begin to age. We are born to be forgotten eventually. We are born to be loved and give love and we are born to lose it or be the loss for someone else. I feel like at birth we should all be given a headstone. As we live, more of our story is etched into the surface. And when we die, people can see more about us. I always wanted a poem carved into mine."

"Which poem?"

"Just something by Robert Frost. A few of the lines from 'Stars'."

"Will you say it to me?"

"Sure." Riley took a deep breath and began to quote the lines slowly. "'As if with keenness for our fate/ Our faltering few steps on/ to white rest, and a place of rest/ Invisible at dawn.' I guess a kind of ironic choice for a girl who has never actually seen stars."

I chuckled a little. "I guess you're right. It's really beautiful though. I just don't want to read that on a stone for a very long time."

"Don't worry about that," she said.

"Will you say to me again?"

"Uh, yeah." So she repeated those lines even slower than she did the first time. I memorized them that time.

"We really should get back now," she said.

"Yeah, we probably should."

I said those lines in my head over and over again.

CHAPTER NINETEEN

When we got back to Riley's house, her mom was asleep on the couch. Her eyes looked a little puffy, as if she had been crying. She probably was crying, honestly. I feel like if your kid is unhappy, the parent is unhappy. Everyone wants their children to be happy, I think. If not, there is something seriously wrong with that parent. Parents have already gone through enough shit, that by the time they have a kid, they never want their child to experience the same things. However, as is the nature of the universe, everyone will experience bad things. If anyone says they haven't, they're lying or have never even lived.

Riley kissed her mom on the cheek and then she and I went into her room. That made me miss my mom and dad. Riley and I went straight to sleep. No drinking. No karaoke. No sharing a toothbrush. No stories. No nothing. Just sleep. We kissed goodnight and fell asleep on her bedroom floor.

That night, I heard Riley talk in her sleep. I wanted to wake her, but she probably wouldn't remember it in the morning, anyway. "No," she said, over and over. "Please, don't go...I'm not...I'm not sleeping, Daddy. Just, just wake me up." I knew that she was probably dreaming about that night she told me about, and I felt so bad for her. Life is bad enough. People deserve good dreams no matter what. She tossed and turned and made sounds like crying even though there were no tears. I wrapped my arms around her and whispered that things were fine.

That I was right beside her. I knew she couldn't hear me, but I did it anyway. She was this girl I barely knew, but I wanted her to be more okay than anyone I knew well.

*   *   *

Riley's phone rang around seven the next morning. She groaned. "Duke, can you get that? It's in my back pocket."

I took her phone from her pocket, and *that's all I did.* I touched nothing else. "Hello?"

"Riley?" I recognized the voiced as Johnny from the show.

"Um, no. She's sleeping. It's Duke. The guy you blew glitter on?" I said, hoping he would remember.

"Oh!" he said after a few seconds. "Yes, you're fabulous and I totally know who you are. I was just confused when I heard your voice. I mean, I know Riley smokes but I didn't think it was getting that bad, yet."

I laughed awkwardly. "Yeah, her voice is still the same. I don't think she smokes that much."

"I suppose not as much as other people."

"Yup." I didn't know what else to say. It was mostly just sort of awkward.

"So, I was just checking on Riley because we have a show tonight. I cannot have the King be hungover or high or anything. She must look marvelous!"

I glanced over at Riley who was snoring ever so slightly. "She looks as beautiful as ever," I said.

"Wonderful, darling." It felt weird to be called darling by another guy, but I went with it. Considering Johnny's gay, it's probably just the weirder equivalent of being called cute by a girl. I just went along with it. I assumed he called all guys darling. Except the guys that pissed him off and refused his sparkles.

"Yeah. I'll have her call you back when she wakes up," I said. "I'm sure she'd like to talk to you."

"Perfect. Hey, are you and Riley a thing?" Johnny asked. "She hardly goes more than a day without calling me. You must be keeping her busy."

"Like, are we dating?"

"Yup."

"Then yes. I think that we're kind of like a thing," I said, and caught myself smiling as I said it.

"She likes you."

"How can you tell?" He had only seen her and me together that one time at the show when we first met.

"Her eyes. They hide a lot of things, you know. But they were different when she saw you that night. We've sparkled a lot of guys and she always just thanks them and sends them away, never speaking to them again. You were different for some reason."

It made me so happy to hear that from someone else.

"I really like her, too. I love her, man."

"That soon? Be careful with that. I don't want to see her hurt."

"I just know. I've never loved anyone like that. Dating was never something I was too worried about. But then I met the most beautiful king. I am hardly worthy of her royalty, but I'm glad she's giving me the chance."

"Did she tell you about…" he said, his voice trailing off. I assumed he knew everything since they seemed like really close friends.

"She told me just about everything."

"Don't ever make her feel that way again."

"I know. I'm trying so hard to help her," I said. I knew she needed one constant in her life. I wanted to be that constant more than I've ever wanted anything. More than I wanted to be the valedictorian of my class. More than I wanted to go to Harvard like my father. More than I wanted to be someone important and famous. More than any of it, I wanted her.

"Good. You're lucky I'm gay or I would've been all up on that a long time ago," he said, laughing. "I mean, damn. She's one sexy king."

"Then it's a very good thing you're gay, huh?"

"Oh, yes." I could hear the expression in his voice and I could almost see the expression on his face to match, as if he were flicking his eyebrows and smirking to himself.

"Well, I guess I'll see you later tonight?"

"Of course. I have another role for you if you're willing."

"Yeah, sure. What should I wear?" I didn't really own anything worthy of a glamorous show.

"I'd ask you to come naked, but that might not go over well with the public. Just wear whatever you wear normally and I'll have something fabulous awaiting the Duke's wonderful arrival. Don't you worry about that."

"I'm excited," I said. Really, I was nervous as hell, but I was telling him what he wanted to hear. And I think that there must have been at least a sliver of excitement in some part of me.

"So am I, dear Duke. There will be enough feathers and glitter for both of us for the rest of our lives. Maybe even a boa. You shall love every second of it. Bye!" And he hung up the phone before I had the chance to respond, which was fine. I wasn't sure how I would have responded to that anyway. I knew that Johnny meant well, but it was still a bit weird to me.

I tossed Riley's phone onto the bed that she never seemed to actually use for sleeping or anything else. "Riley," I whispered, rubbing her back softly. She just rolled over and pulled a blanket over her head.

"God, leave me alone. Sleeping," she said.

"I'm not God. Not even close."

"Fuck off."

"Fine," I said.

"Sorry. I meant that as lovingly as possible." She sat up and yawned. Her breath was awful, but mine was probably worse. "Who called?"

"It was your dearest Queen."

"Jesus Christ, I completely forgot about tonight."

"I'm not Jesus, either. You seriously give me way too much credit."

She laughed. "You're probably right."

"Always."

"It's a good thing we didn't drink last night or I'd be totally fucked."

"You kinda handle drinking better than I do," I admitted.

"Is that so?"

"Yup. I'm just not fond of the taste."

"I'm pretty sure nobody sits there and downs a bottle of whiskey thinking, 'This is the greatest thing I have ever tasted.' That's just not how it works. It's not for taste. It's for pain."

"Yeah, I guess so. Beer is just like drinking the fermented juice of random wheat plants or whatever. That sounds kind of disgusting."

"But doesn't smoking sound just as bad? Like what sounds appealing about breathing in the smoke of a hundred chemicals for years until your lungs become black and sticky and cancer forms in places you didn't know you had? Nothing that people love and are addicted to is generally good. We feel pain, so we do things that numb the pain for a little while just to cause more harm to ourselves later. The cycle of the thoughts of people is pretty jacked up, if you ask me."

"Jacked up is a good way to describe every single person who has ever existed," I said. "But there are risks to even the most wonderful feelings."

"Like love?" Riley asked.

"Exactly like love," I said. "When you love, there is always that risk of losing the greatest thing you've ever had."

"Yeah."

"Yeah."

"I'm scared," she said. I didn't know what exactly she was afraid of. Maybe afraid of trusting someone else again.

"Me, too." But I wouldn't say that I was scared in a bad way. I was scared in the way that I realized that I finally had something it would kill me to lose.

Out of nowhere Riley reached to grab a pillow and hit right upside the head with it.

"Oh, so you're going to be like that, are you?" I grabbed the pillow I was using and hit her back.

Thus began the most ultimate pillow fight.

We ran around her room whacking each other and cracking up with laughter. We stood on her bed as we fought. I knocked her down onto the mattress. "You might have won this battle, Duke, but I will have my revenge," Riley said. Then she stuck out her tongue in a very poor attempt at playing dead.

"Never!" I shouted and hit her one more time.

Riley laughed and sat up. "You are such a dork."

"And so are you, my dear. That just proved everything. But don't worry. I shall not tell any of your subjects. I know you have a reputation to maintain."

CHAPTER TWENTY

Riley and I killed the hours we had before the show started by sitting in a park and watching people in a way that was purely observational and non-creepish. Riley and I were so much alike and it was wonderful in every way. Yet we were different enough so that we never got bored of each other. It was perfect how that worked out. We both shared things and had our own unique things to contribute, she more so than I. As we sat there just seeing people for who they might have been, our perspectives were so different—Riley's from a view of understanding and relativity, since she had lived in Las Vegas her entire life, and mine from a view of wonder and curiosity. I was on the outside looking in. There was a haze over my eyes. But Riley saw through it, because she was on the other side.

I pointed out that there was a fountain in the center of the park, and from where we were sitting, we could see it perfectly. A little girl was begging her grandparents for a coin to toss into that fountain, which in her mind had been idealized as a beautiful wishing well, capable of making all of her dreams comes true. I couldn't hear her, but I could tell by the way that she was tugging on her grandfather's sleeve. Nobody could deny a child their wish, so he did give her a coin. Riley and I watched as the girl faced away from the fountain, closed her eyes, and tossed the coin over her head. She turned back around just in time to watch the coin break the surface of the water. She laughed and clapped and her grandma smiled, no doubt a response to the girl's simple happiness and innocence. "What do you think she wished for?" I asked.

"Love," Riley said.

"Really?" I would have said something like a pony or cotton candy or something like that. Things that I assumed little girls liked. Hell, even I liked cotton candy.

"Yeah. I don't think she wished for some sexy dude to just rise from the water all dripping and iridescent in the sun like the merman every girl dreams of," she laughed. "But I think she wished for something like her dog to be alive again or for her best friend to move back home. Those are things thought of and wished for in love, whether or not we realize it at the time." Christ, I was so incredibly superficial compared to her. I don't know how she didn't see it.

"I hope I can be everything you ever wished for, even though I'm not particularly a sexy merman. If you want, I can give you a coin and you can go wish for my fabulous merman beauty, if you prefer."

"I'm pretty okay with your awkwardly scrawny self. I wouldn't say I ever wished for this kind of love, but I'm glad I have it."

"So do I," I said. Then, "I kind of feel bad for little kids sometimes. But I also envy them."

"And why is that?"

"They are in this bubble that takes all shit in the world and makes it invisible, you know? They're so happy and unaware of everything bad around them. One day, that protective barrier of happiness will pop, and that little girl over there will never know what hit her. Sometimes you have to wonder if it's better to be naïve and sheltered from harm or to just see it clearly for what it is. They both have their own goodness."

"That, my friend, is one of life's many awful truths."

I nodded in agreement. Riley went on to note an elderly couple sitting on a bench like we were. "I wonder what their story is," she said.

"You do love stories."

"I just think that people deserve to live longer than they actually do."

"Well, what do you think their lives tell?" I asked.

"It's hard to say. Look at us. We're probably seventy years younger than they are, but we are doing the exact same thing. Maybe they've been watching people in the park since they were our age. Or perhaps this park is their favorite place in the world because this is where they were engaged, and they think every day could be it. The day of the last day. And if they just sit in this park for as long as they can for the remainder of their final days, maybe they can die where they were the most happy."

"A little morbid, but romantic, too. If that does happen to be the case, we'll be performing burlesque for the rest of our lives. That means many more years of feathers and glitter and Johnny dressing us up like rather inappropriate dolls."

She laughed softly. "As long as I'm with you until the foundations crumble beyond repair."

"The crumbling foundations of a crooked kingdom's crooked king." I saw her smile at the reference I made.

And that is how we spent those few hours, pointing out anything from young Goth couples to joggers to middle-aged men walking their dogs and not cleaning up after them. A few Jesus-freaks walked up to us and gave us booklets asking where we would go when all the world is consumed in flames and oblivion. I curtly replied, "Wherever the fuck I want to go. This pamphlet doesn't control anything." And then Riley laughed so hard as she told them to go fuck themselves. They walked away without another word, probably whispering silent prayers in their hearts for the worst of these sinners. I was surprised that Christians would even settle in Vegas, anyway. She and I stood and tossed the little pamphlets in the fountain, which was probably littering. But who the hell cares? I didn't. Neither did she.

"And that is exactly why I don't go to church," Riley said. "I just want to live one goddamn day without being confronted about death in some way. I was perfectly content in my subconscious human brevity, but then they have to come along and act like the world is ending tomorrow. Fuck that."

"I know what you mean. Church is kinda bleak. I went with my grandma one Easter when I was probably nine. It was the worst experience of my life. The guy droned on and on about how we all need to confess our sins and, if we don't, our souls will burn and be eaten by worms in hell's unquenchable flame. That sure does sound like a loving God to me. I'm just sticking with being a good person and I'll see what happens after that."

"I totally agree with everything you just said. However, if going to church one time was the worst experience of your life, I'd trade you in a heartbeat," she said.

"Riley, you know that's not what I meant. It's just an expression used too often." But she was right. I hadn't really gone through a whole lot.

"Forget it."

"I'm sorry, okay?"

"Yeah."

"I love you so much," I said. "I really do."

"And I love you. Sorry I reacted that way. I shouldn't want people to have shitty lives because my one attempt at existence sucks. That's kind of bitchy."

"Hey, don't worry about it," I said. Even her little smirk was gone this time. Because we happened to be beside the fountain, I decided to splash her a little.

Okay, it was a lot. But it was just water.

"You did not just do that!" she said. I saw the smile coming back.

"Um, yeah. I believe I did just do that."

I expected her to splash me back, but her move was much bolder than anticipated. She actually shoved me into the fountain. I was completely taken off guard.

"Jesus Christ, Riley." And she was actually laughing in the best way. Whatever it took to see her that way, I was more than okay with it.

"Are you praying?" she asked rather sarcastically. "You're letting their words of idiocy grow on you."

"Not at all," I said, standing up from the water. I felt so extremely heavy. "Give me a hug, babe. I've already forgiven you."

"You will never catch me," she shouted, and took off running. "I told you I would have my revenge!"

"I'll catch up. Don't you worry about that." I forced my legs to move faster despite the extra weight, but Riley was pretty quick. She was running through the grass and I saw her glance over her shoulder twice. She finally started to slow down and I used my last ounce of wavering energy to sneak behind her. I grabbed her from behind and pulled her down with we onto the grass. My clothes were still soaked and she freaked out when I touched her.

"Your skin is freezing," she said, laughing and breathing hard.

"My skin's actually pretty warm. It's just the shirt." So I took it off and laid on my back in the cool grass. "The fountain was surprisingly cold considering how hot it is out here."

Riley rested her head on my chest, her fiery hair just slightly damp. "I think everyone in Vegas has seen a drunk guy running around naked at least once or twice in their life. This is nothing."

I leaned my head down to kiss her. "No," I said. "This is everything."

"You're right," she said and kissed me back.

"I'll never hear you say that again."

"You might be right again," she said through soft laughter.

"Maybe."

"We should probably head over to the theatre," she said. "Johnny will kill me if we're late."

"We can't have that," I said, smiling. "Besides, when I talked to him earlier, he seemed really excited about my outfit and possible boa."

Riley rolled her eyes playfully. "I absolutely cannot wait to see that."

"Johnny is probably thinking the exact same thing right about now."

CHAPTER TWENTY-ONE

Riley and I walked to the theatre and made it with seven minutes to spare. "He's with me," Riley told that same emotionless girl that Luke, Bryce, and I encountered when we first happened across the show. Her eyeliner was still very heavily applied and again she was smacking her gum obnoxiously, as if there was no other way that one could enjoy gum. I imagine that if she actually ever smiled her teeth would have been stained a permanent color of bubblegum pink.

"Whatever," she said. "Does it look like I care?"

We didn't respond to that. She obviously did not.

Johnny was backstage and absolutely freaking out. "What the hell is your problem? We are on in five! Riley, in all the time we have been doing this show, you have never once been late. Don't let this boy get to you. King, you know what to wear. Duke, go into the corner and change into this." He tossed me a garbage bag. "I'll try not to watch you." And then he winked at me. "

"Okay," I said.

"And try to hurry just a little. Please and thanks a bunch," he said.

"Where are Scarlet and Ginger?" Riley asked while shimmying into her feathered skirt.

"Getting the beer from my car," Johnny said. "Because they actually know *how to show up on time.*"

"Fuck you," she said. "It was one effing time."

"Fuck you," he said back. "One time is all it takes to ruin a show."

Johnny was really hardcore about burlesque, apparently.

I found their conversation amusing, because I know their "fuck you" was meant with the most endearment possible. However, I really needed to figure out my costume. I wasn't given any pants, but a sequined Speedo thing. I wanted to run away right then, but I fought the urge and put them on.

I really had scrawny-ass legs. I pulled out what I thought was a blanket for whatever reason. It actually turned out to be a robe that barely went to my knees. It looked like something Santa would wear. That is, if Santa were a male stripper every day of the year except for one. Perhaps that was why Mrs. Clause stayed with him.

At the very bottom was a pink boa that didn't match the rest of my clothes, but I'd definitely say it was very, super gay. I knew I looked completely ridiculous, but I stepped away from my Corner of Shame. I walked up to Johnny. "How do I look?"

He squealed in nothing but pure delight. "You look fabulous! But not yet perfect. I have one more thing." He took his hands from behind his back to reveal an honest-to-God tiara. He put it on my head with all the seriousness of a coronation.

"There! You are the most gorgeous Duke Las Vegas has had or will ever have."

"Uh, thank you."

"You, dear, are so welcome."

Then there was really loud laughter. It was Riley a few feet away.

"Is it that bad?" I asked.

"No. No, not at all," she said, still laughing.

"Then what?"

"It's just that you are so straight and Johnny is so gay. You are probably dying inside, aren't you?"

"Actually, I feel more alive than ever. Except for maybe thirty minutes ago," I said, smiling at Riley. Her eyebrows flicked up and I knew she was thinking exactly what I was thinking.

"Stop eye flirting! There is no time for this," Johnny said.

Scarlet and Ginger walked up to us with a cooler. "Hope it's enough. It's packed tonight," Ginger said. By packed she meant, like, sixty-five people.

"It'll be enough," Johnny assured us. "It's show time. Break a leg, everyone!" he said in a melodic voice.

We took deep breaths (me more than the others) and did those overly dramatic but apparently theatrical jazz hand things and Scarlet spoke the usual lines into the microphone.

You heard that Vegas is just drugs and sex.
But you've never seen the Lost Burlesque.

Then half the audience joined. I recognized a few of the people from last time.

You know Scarlet and Ginger and Johnny the Queen,
But they better move over for Riley King.

I was completely surprised by what Scarlet said next.

Oh, wait! There's more. It's not a fluke.
We're introducing Wade the Duke.

There were a few shouts from the audience and my heart was racing. Riley took my hand. "Let's go."

"Did you know about that?"

"The King knows everything that happens in her jurisdiction, baby."

We stood in the center of the stage, the lights warming our already-hot skin. "How are my subjects tonight?" Riley shouted. Everyone just screamed in response. I looked out and wondered how many were there for the first time by just some chance like me. Riley took off her robe and let it fall to the floor, revealing the skirt and bikini top beneath. The guys whistled and the girls rolled their eyes. I saw a couple girls punch the arms of their boyfriends in a way that the guys took as casually playful but that the girls meant with the fire of a thousand hells.

Me? I was just breath-taken by everything about her. From the very beginning, I never saw her the way other guys did. I didn't look at her and lust after her in that way. I just saw her. *Her.* How stunning she was. Remarkably unique. As I learned about her more, her beauty only intensified. When I saw her scars, I didn't see her as imperfect. I saw her as someone who was wounded but healed stronger than ever.

"All the world's a stage, and its men and women merely players," Riley said. I recognized Shakespeare's quote immediately. When she said that, Johnny came out and placed the crown on her head. "Let my people drink!" she said. On either side of the stage, Ginger and Scarlet handed each person a warm beer, not caring about whether or not they were twenty-one. They poured the extra on Riley and I. Johnny kissed both of us and licked the beer off our skin. I wasn't jealous when he kissed Riley. It was like a girl kissing another girl on the cheek, like they do in movies sometimes upon leaving each other for a few hours.

Johnny gave me the bag of glitter and I knew what to do. I walked back and forth across the stage. There were four guys on the front row. I made eye contact with each one of them. Two looked away in under three seconds. I chose this blonde kid who honestly looked like he was twelve, but he was drinking anyway. Without saying a word, I held his gaze and he never looked away. I held out my palm, blew the glitter on his face as Johnny did to me not long before. One his friends laughed at him and said he looked like a faggot. It was definitely their first time to the show.

"You, sir," I said. "Come join us on this stage and dance among the royal family of Las Vegas!"

He stood up and started to climb up to the stage. Then a phone rang backstage and he seemed unsure of what to do.

I didn't know whether or not it was planned, but Riley went right along with it.

"Uh, it appears that somebody has called for the king," she said, as poised as she could. She ran backstage and there was only silence. Silence. Silence.

"Riley?" I said. More silence. Then the worst sound I have ever heard. She just screamed and screamed and everything about it was raw and unrehearsed. The audience just kind of looked around at nothing in particular. Nobody was really sure of what was going on. They knew as much as we did. I heard her phone drop to the floor and she started crying in the worst possible way.

I ran backstage and closed the curtain. I could hear Johnny trying to keep the people calm by joking around, but I knew he must have been as terrified, if not more, than I was. Riley was curled up on the floor and I could hear a voice coming from her phone. "Miss? Miss, are you alright?"

I picked it up. "What the fuck is going on?" I didn't care who was on the other end. Something was very wrong and I needed to know.

"I am going to need you to calm down, sir. Who am I speaking to?" a voice said slowly.

"The girl you called. I'm her boyfriend. Who is this?"

"My name is Officer Alexander."

Then I knew something was more wrong than I ever could have imagined. "Just please tell me what's going on. Please."

"Miss King's mother was involved in a serious accident. I am so sorry to have to tell you this, but she died at the scene. The autopsy has not yet been performed, but I was there and I did smell alcohol on her breath. I believe she was intoxicated well above the legal limit."

"No no no. God, no. She doesn't need this shit! Her mother is all she has left. Please tell me you're wrong." My last few words were just a whisper. "Please tell me this is some kind of a sick joke." But I knew it wasn't. Nobody would joke about something like that.

"I'm very sorry for your loss, sir. Is there anything I can do for you and your friend?" the cop asked.

"If you can't fix this, don't bother with anything else." I hung up the phone and sat on the floor beside Riley, but not looking at her. There was absolutely nothing I could do to help her, and I was scared. I didn't know what to do and she needed to feel something besides pain again for once in her life. She wouldn't stop crying. She couldn't. I held her tightly, though she didn't respond. I went through the night when she told me her story and when we sang terrible karaoke and sang her the only song I could bring to mind. It was an old song by The Smiths. It was the first time I heard it and I downloaded it that same night. I had never heard it, but she knew every word.

Sing me to sleep. Sing me to sleep.
I'm tired and I, I want to go to bed.
Don't feel bad for me. I want you to know,
Deep in the cell of my heart I really want to go.

Those were the only words I knew, so I sang those few lines like a broken record. She never looked at me and she never stopped crying until she fell asleep on the floor backstage. It was her stage, and there she was, collapsed onto it. I didn't have anything else I could do, so I kept singing.

CHAPTER TWENTY-TWO

After the show, which mostly consisted of shallow impromptu skits, Ginger and Scarlet walked home and Johnny drove Riley and me to her house. Johnny tried to cheer her up some, but nothing was working. She fell back asleep on the short drive home. I was hesitant to wake her up because sleep was the only way to forget sometimes, unless the reality carried over into her dreams. I was praying to something that her dreams would at least be a safe place for her to go.

I walked her to the door and she didn't say anything. She was as lifeless as any living person could be. It was so scary. We sat on the couch for hours doing absolutely nothing. Riley wasn't crying anymore. She was probably numbed to world. No pain. No sadness. No happiness. Just an empty shell. My arms were around her and I never let her go. I needed her to feel something, even if it was just her knowing that I was beside her the entire time. She needed to know that I was never, ever going to leave her alone in this world.

The hospital called a while later and verified what the officer assumed, telling me that Riley's mom was very intoxicated. I tried to give Riley the phone but she only shook her head. After a couple minutes I just gave up. Another hour seemed to drag on before she finally spoke. They weren't words I wanted to hear. "Every kingdom there ever was has fallen. Every king has been dethroned. Nothing so perfect can last forever. You know that, too." Then she walked away and I heard her shut her bedroom door. I assumed that she just wanted to be along with her own thoughts for a while. I didn't follow her. God, I should have ran after her without a second thought. I thought that maybe she just needed to be alone. But maybe if you love someone, you follow them anyway. I did love her. I do love her.

Like fifteen minutes later I went to check on her. She was really quiet, so I thought that maybe she had fallen back asleep. I wanted to curl up beside her and just be there for her. I turned her doorknob, but it was locked. Then I started to panic. I knew why her mom never allowed Riley to lock her bedroom door. I knocked. "Riley?"

And then she laughed her nervous laugh, but it was very different. It wasn't *her.* "She'll be gone soon," Riley whispered. I could barely make out the words she said.

I pounded on the door harder, slamming my entire body into it. "Riley, don't do this! Please. Let me in. I love you. Do not do this. You cannot leave me like this. Don't go." And I knew that I was being so selfish. She had no reason to stay. Not for me. I could never make her that happy again. "There was so much we were supposed to do, remember? Remember the karaoke our first night together? We were supposed to see The Killers again together. You have to get their signatures again. Please. I love you." I could hear my voice cracking, but I didn't want her to hear it. I wanted to be strong for her.

"I love you, too. I'm sorry. I'll miss you if I can." The last sentence was hardly a murmur. "I really hope that I can."

I tried and tried to knock the door down, but it wouldn't budge. I kept screaming her name but she didn't answer. I was so scared. I fell onto the floor and just broke down. That was the first time I had ever cried so much and so hard. I found someone it would kill me to lose. I would rather die than lose her. I felt everything inside my body just crumble into millions of tiny pieces. My heart had imploded into nothing but dust. I couldn't feel. I didn't know what was happening. I was so happy and then it was gone. I leaned against her door. I hit my head against it over and over again. I sat there and whispered her name out loud, hoping that she would answer me. "Riley, Riley Riley…"

I felt such hatred for myself for not going after. I could have stopped her. I could have been holding her in that moment. I could have whispering into her ear that I love her so very much. But there was nothing to be done.
I called for an ambulance instead of 911 because I knew it was too late. She couldn't be saved. I told them that they didn't have to hurry because I knew she was gone.

The paramedics were able to break down the door. I asked them if they could stay behind so I could see her first. One of the men said that wasn't a good idea, but his partner said it was okay. "Thank you," I said. "I promise that it won't take very long."

They waited in the living room. I walked into Riley's room and I actually saw the story she told me such a short time ago. But one thing was different. This ending was permanent. It could never be edited in any way at all. I laid on the floor beside her just like we always used to do. There was blood on the carpet that would mask the old stains with the new. There was so much of it. Her skin smelled like the cheap beer from the shows. Her skin that was always so pale but nearly transparent. Her blood that no longer sustained her life stained my clothes. It wasn't real. But at the same time, it was more real than anything I have ever felt. I wanted to unfeel everything about it, but that would mean I'd have to unknow every single part of it.

That would mean I would have to unknow Riley King. I didn't want that. I needed to hold on to her as long as possible. I missed her like hell already.

I walked back into the living room where the paramedics were standing silently. I looked at them and I nodded. There were tears running down my cheeks and falling from my chin onto my shirt. My tears mixed with Riley's blood.

"I'm sorry, kid. It must be really hard," one of the men said.

I just nodded. He had no idea.

A few minutes later, I watched them carry Riley outside in a body bag with a stretcher. They didn't say anything else to me. I stood in the doorway and saw them load her body into the back of an ambulance.

And it hurt so badly.

CHAPTER TWENTY-THREE

Riley King died one year ago today. She didn't take her own life, because I don't think that anybody really desires death. People just want to be happy. We just want things to be better. The kingdom took the life of its crooked but perfect ruler. I walk to the LVC after dusk and I don't care if I am caught. I have to talk to her. I walk past the tomb that holds my memories just as much as it holds those bodies inside it. I walk through endless rows of the dead. I think how much Riley would want to write their untold stories.

Riley's gravesite is nothing that remarkable. Nothing about it would make someone stop and wonder about her. It's small and I know many people have seen it without wondering the story of the girl who died so young. I know there are countless lives that were cut shorter than hers, but she was still young and so incredible and deserved so much more time.

I can tell you her story, but I can never tell it as honestly as the way she lived it. I kneel over her grave and cry. That night, I was no more than six feet from her when she was doing it. She was so close to me. But now six feet feels like a terribly far distance, as unfathomable as millions of miles. "Why did you do this to me?" I say. My words are broken. "Fuck you," I say. I always say that to her, but I can't be mad at her. Then, as always, I apologize. "I—I'm so sorry, Riley. I love you so much and I am still so scared." I don't know what I am afraid of, exactly.

I think I'm afraid of never seeing her again. I don't know what I believe in about an afterlife and shit like that. I can be hopeful. I can be realistic. I haven't talked with my parents in about a year. I walk back home and I decide to write them a letter. I live in Riley's house. So many of her stories are written on those walls. I want to keep them around. She would like that, I think. I don't go into detail in the letter. I write enough to give them the idea of what happened. I knew that they were probably still so worried about me.

I wanted to give them something to let them know that I was okay.

I think.

Dear Mom and Dad,

I lied to you about a few things. Well, that was another lie. I lied to you about everything. I know that you both wanted the best for me. I always appreciated that, even if it didn't always seem like I did. I swear to God I did. That is not a lie.

You both knew me so well. Or you thought you did. I didn't even really know myself more than anyone else did. I was the son every parent could have asked for, wasn't I? I know you think so, but I wasn't. I'm not. And I am so sorry. So much of my life was lived as a mere clone of what you wanted me to be. For the longest time, I believed that the shallow clone was really me. I did what I did to make you guys happy, and I was losing sight of my own happiness in the process.

I can't tell you where I am right now or why I didn't go to school. I can't guarantee that you will see me again. Just don't worry about me. Please don't do that.

When I made the decision to live my own life, it wasn't easy. I can't tell you how many times I regretted it and wanted to turn around. But two people who used to be my best friends never would have let me live it down, and I am so grateful for that. For the first time in as long as I can remember, I felt alive in more ways than just breathing and being. My heart was beating for something and someone. In every breath was the sweet and sometimes cigarette-tinged scent of the most beautiful soul that has ever been and will ever be.

She deserved so much better than this world. I would have fought the armies of heaven and hell to protect her. I let her down and I am so, so sorry. God, I love her so much. I miss her. I have a couple pictures of her on my phone, but it hurts to look at them sometimes. But I stare at them anyway. When I look at the pictures, I see her, but I don't see *her*. I don't ever want to forget what we had. She was just...perfect. There is no other way to describe her.

She was so smart. Maybe even smarter than me. But she didn't know it. I should have worked harder to convince her. What if I fucked up? She'd punch my arm if she saw me crying right now. I don't think she can, but the thought of her seeing me like this is far better than the thought of her not seeing anything. Of her not existing in some dark, void, infinite blackness. If that is the reality, it is much too hard to think about until I face it one day. She faced it too soon.

I would have taken her hand in death and followed her to the edge of the blackness and even beyond that. If I could start over, I promise that I would do so much better. I would have saved her.

You know that time around six in the evening in October when the sun has set but it isn't completely dark yet and everything in the world is the same shade of blue for a little while? That is how I feel. She was my light and she is gone. But somehow, the darkness is not complete. I'm just trying my hardest to distinguish the shades now.

The crooked king fell before her kingdom. I want to fall with her and never get up again. Nothing is left. She was my everything. I know she would want me to be happy. One day, I'll try.

The Duke

ACKNOWLEDGEMENTS

I would like to thank everyone who has been involved in this book from start to finish.

Thank you first to my publisher, Makin Books, and everyone on the team for welcoming me to their literary family and giving me such a wonderful opportunity to share my story with the world. I am very lucky to be able to work with such great people.

Thank you to my fiancé, Franklin, who has always been there to support me and my love of writing. You are always there to read the messy rough drafts I produce, and this book was no exception. I have no doubt that I could not have made it this far without your love and encouragement.

Thank you to my mom who helped me get started in writing this book. From the hand-written first draft, to the edits on my tablet, and to the typing that I would do late at night on her laptop (often without her permission) when I should have been asleep. Love you, Mom.

Thank you to Ava Dellaira and Gregory Galloway, two fantastic writers with whom I have spoken and learned from. Their words of experience have been a great help in this journey and it has been a privilege to know them.

Thank you to my favorite writers and musicians who have for sure been an influence in my writing. John Green and The Airborne Toxic Event, to name a couple.

And lastly, thank you to my friends who have always been so supportive of what I do: Robbie, Maddie, James. You guys rock.

Alex Katt

Made in the USA
San Bernardino, CA
25 August 2016